Tennessee Renegade

Bucky Enderby was just sixteen years old when he had to flee his native Tennessee for killing three men.

After going to war he ran with outlaws spawned by that conflict. But soon he found himself riding the lonely trails again, looking for something he couldn't put a name to. Kim Preece had at least part of that 'something' and he tried to settle down.

But the newly-revived Texas Rangers beckoned and he crossed the Rio to find a wild kid worth thousands in reward money. There were men who aimed to claim that money – but first they would have to get past Enderby's guns.

By the same author

Shoot on Sight
Hellfire Pass
Blood Kin
The Cougar Canyon Run
Travis Quinn, Outlaw
Bronco Madigan
Cimarron Arrow
Madigan's Star
Count Your Bullets
Madigan's Lady
Bull's-Eye
Madigan's Sidekick

Tennessee Renegade

HANK J. KIRBY

ROBERT HALE · LONDON

© Hank J. Kirby 2005
First published in Great Britain 2005

ISBN 0 7090 7640 1

Robert Hale Limited
Clerkenwell House
Clerkenwell Green
London EC1R 0HT

The right of Hank J. Kirby to be identified as author of this work has been asserted by him in accordance with the Copyright, Designs and Patents Act 1988.

All characters and events in this book are fictitious and any resemblance to any real person or circumstance is unintentional

Typeset by
Derek Doyle & Associates, Liverpool.
Printed and bound in Great Britain by
Antony Rowe Limited, Wiltshire

PROLOGUE

1861

Bucky Enderby ran through the damp brush, leaves and twigs from the green branches whipping at his young face. He ignored this although he felt the flesh tear and begin to bleed in several places.

The long Kentucky hunting rifle that had belonged to his grandfather trailed from his right hand, impeding his progress a little, but he knew he was going to need it in a few minutes and hoped the rain-wet leaves hadn't caused the home-ground gun powder to cake and so make it hard to ignite. Panting, long straw-coloured hair flapping around his ears and across his eyes, he staggered out of the brush on to the side of the knoll overlooking the secret hollow where Pa and his older brothers ran their still.

'Too late! Goldarn it! I'm way too late!' He was a little young to cuss, not that he didn't know the words, but Ma had been a stickler for decent language and he had had his mouth washed out twice with her lye soap. Once should have been enough.

Now, catching laboured breaths, he stood just behind a huckleberry bush and watched the men moving about below.

Pa was lying stretched out on the ground and he could see the smear of blood matting his hair from up here. Cole was sitting with his back against a tree, mouth slack, rained-on hair in his face, one hand clawing a bloody patch on his homespun shirt. Jared was nursing a bullet-shattered leg just outside the crude sheet-iron shelter that held the still.

There were three men under that shelter, two he knew would be the Revenue agents brought out here by the third man, Sheriff Asa Hunsecker. He said he would square with Pa for licking him after the last Turkey Shoot in front of the whole of the folk who lived in the Big Smokies and also some Kentuckians who had come across the State Line for the festivities. This was the lawman's way of doing it, betraying the Enderbys to the Revenue men.

'You son of a bitch, Hunsecker!' Bucky Enderby sobbed as he dug deep in the pockets of his torn trousers and found the wadded rag and piece of chamois. He swiftly wiped over the gun-breech and hammer, took out the percussion caps carefully wrapped in the chamois and thumbed one on to the nipple. The hammer cocked smoothly beneath his surprisingly steady thumb and he worked the beautifully curved burr-walnut stock and butt into a comfortable position, getting down on one knee.

The rain drumming on the sheet-iron roof above

the still as Hunsecker and the Revenue men started to wreck it drowned the crisp whipcrack as the long-barrelled rifle fired, its woodwork absorbing much of the recoil. The .41 calibre ball took Hunsecker across the face, cutting open the left side like the blade of a knife. The lawman screamed and spun into the hot still, hands sizzling against the heated copper tubes. He convulsed and screamed again as he pushed himself off and fell to his knees. His head was in his hands and Bucky could hear the howling he set up way back here.

The Revenue men, intent on smashing Pa's still, didn't know what had happened. They hadn't heard the gunshot, but they soon saw the damage it had done to Asa Hunsecker's face, never too handsome at the best of times, but now forever marked to remind him for the rest of his life that a 16-year-old backwoods kid had taken revenge for his treachery.

By now, Bucky had reloaded and whipped the ramrod out of the long barrel as the Revenue men drew their cumbersome revolvers and fired blindly up the slope, not knowing where he was. The second shot didn't give them his position either. It caught them half-turned away, the ball taking the gun clear out of the first agent's hands with a dull clunking sound as the lead flattened against the blued steel of the revolver's frame. The man lurched and cursed and the ricocheting bullet burned across the hip of his companion standing next to him. The man toppled like a Saturday-night drunk and Jared whooped like a brush turkey at mating time.

'Nail 'em, young'un!' he croaked, his voice hoarse

and weak with the pain in him, it looked like the big artery in his thigh had been severed by the bullet he had taken. 'Finish it, Bucky! Pa's gone and so's Cole . . . I'll be joinin' 'em right soon . . . You knows what to . . . do—'

'Shut up, you stinkin' moonshiner!' snarled the Revenue man whose gun had been torn from his grasp. He stooped and picked up his companion's revolver. Bucky sobbed with effort, trying to ram the third ball down the long barrel, jamming the iron ramrod in his haste. Tears blurred his vision. His ears were ringing with Jared's words – *You know what to do!* – well, he did know what to do. It had been hammered into him many a time: 'If the Revenue men come they'll come a'shooting and that means someone's going to die. Don't let them leave alive, blow up the still if need be—' *He could hear Pa's voice now. . . .*

That was the Enderby Code: give the Revenue agents *nothing* in the way of evidence. They hated the hill men, killed on sight, never even differentiating between men and women and, a few times, children.

Bucky jumped at the thumping roar of the big revolver below and, the ramrod freed at last as he pushed the ball home on its charge of powder, he saw that the agent with the numbed hand had shot Jared through the head. Choking now, Bucky thumbed home the percussion cap, cocking the hammer as he lifted the long rifle to his shoulder. He had the sight on the killer's head, but on seeing Hunsecker on hands and knees, crawling out of the still shed towards some rocks, he changed his point of aim.

He fired into the big copper tank bubbling above the flames, hitting the seam perfectly. It split the tank like a blow from some giant axe, and spilled the sour-mash into the firepit. The exploding tank ripped loose the condenser tubing to the reservoir of almost pure alcohol, and it too spewed into the firepit.

He had a brief vision of blue-tongued flames leaping back up the flooding stream into the complex distillation system and then everything dissolved in a raging, rolling, expanding ball of flame that hurtled across the hollow a blink-of-an-eye ahead of a thunderclap worthy of Judgement Day.

Bucky Enderby was blown off his feet. The huckleberry bush and those surrounding it were stripped of their leaves and fruit. Saplings twisted and whipped into fantastic corkscrew shapes around him. Dirt filled the air like buckshot. Mangled sheet-iron and sheared copper and brass whistled and howled and thudded deep into the slope.

Something straight out of Hell seemed to roll right over Bucky's thin, gangling body and his ears rang and whistled until he couldn't get his bearings. The hollow was filled with fire and the forest was starting to burn. Somehow he got his shaky legs under him, found the long rifle and his possible sack with his powder-flask and spare balls, and staggered back over the crest.

His family was gone now. Ma had gone to glory two years ago. Sister Kate had married and went to live in Georgia, but they had never heard from her, and Pa had decided long, long ago that she had died from the Spanish Fever that had swept that State at the time. Now Pa and Cole and Jared were gone, too.

He had killed a lawman and two Revenue men and he was only four days past his sixteenth birthday.

And he was alone in the world and didn't know what to do. . . .

CHAPTER 1

HOME IS THE HUNTER
1875

The girl standing in the doorway of the ranch house with the rifle cradled firmly in her arms watched the rider slow down by the corrals and then stop and dismount.

Her mouth thinned into a hard, straight slash and her dark eyes slitted.

'A whole year late and you come back wounded again!'

She spoke aloud but only loud enough for herself to hear. She tightened her grip on the rifle, watched the man sag against the horse, head down across his arm as he still clutched the saddle horn. He was gasping for breath after the simple process of dismounting. She felt the brief wave of anxiety sweep over her – *How bad was he hurt this time?* – but forced it down and allowed the surge of rising hot anger to wash over her, drowning the stomach-knotting anxiety she had been fighting these last ten days, watching constantly for his return.

'I see you're hurt,' she called quietly.

He lifted his head and his hat fell off, revealing the sweat-damp, wheat-coloured hair, thick and bunched at the base of his neck. His face was deeply tanned and drawn with pain and exhaustion. *God he was thin!* She saw the paleness of his bright blue eyes, and the tautness in his wide mouth that showed through several days' growth of yellow stubble.

He nodded and when he spoke his voice was harsh, strained. 'You gonna help me up to the house. . . ?'

She straightened, stared a moment, then turned back and passed through the doorway into the shaded cool of the parlour.

'I'll get water and bandages ready.'

He swore softly and managed to toss the rein-ends over the middle rail of the corral and twist the rawhide strips around once or twice. It would hold the weary black and keep him from the water-trough until he cooled down. He let the saddle fall and slid his rifle out of the scabbard, worked free the ties on his war bag and let it drop. Breathing heavily, right arm pressed tightly against the blood-stained cloth of his shirt, he fumbled the rifle and got a grip on the war bag strap. He dragged it towards the house, each scrape along the gravel marking his progress.

The girl came back to the door, walked out to the top of the short steps leading up to the porch, watching his efforts as he staggered towards her. She had thick raven-black hair that was long enough to blow a couple of strands across her unseamed forehead. The dark eyes were still narrowed but there was a softness that briefly appeared and she sighed, went down the steps and took the rifle from him, then steadied his arm with her other hand.

'I ought to let you crawl all the way!'

He turned his gaunt face towards her and his lips stretched out in a smile. 'You wouldn't be so cruel, Kim. Just ain't in you.'

'I'm finding it easier and easier to think that way,' she told him shortly and helped him up the steps.

He was near exhaustion by the time they had reached the big, cool kitchen with its slate-flagged floor and the chair rocked when he dropped into it, grunting in pain.

'Where is it this time?' she asked, already tugging his grimy shirt out of his waistband. 'Oh, for heavens sake, drop that damn gunbelt so I can work on you!'

Actually, she unbuckled the belt, noting the many empty bullet loops and how few shells remained. The gun thudded heavily and she loosened his trouser belt, then she impatiently ripped his shirt open, the buttons popping.

'Hey!'

'Oh, shut up! It's too ragged and filthy to wash or even attempt repair. Getting like its owner, maybe!'

She stood back, grimacing despite herself when she saw the dark blood caking the crude wadded neckerchief he had tied over his wound. The gash was deep, the lips swollen, and she saw the raised and bruised welt of flesh going several inches to one side.

He almost jumped out of the chair when she touched it.

'The bullet's still in there!' She said it accusingly.

He was very pale now, blood starting to ooze from the hole. 'Looks like it's skidded around a rib. It'll have to come out! Oh God, Buck! I could kill you myself! Why do you do it? Why do you insist on taking on these – these damn *jobs* as you call them, and keep coming back to me to dig out bullets or sew up knife wounds, splint a broken arm or leg? When is it going to end? Can you tell me that, Buck Enderby? *When in the name of all that's holy is it going to end!*'

She flung herself across the room to where she had an iron kettle steaming on the wood range, her teeth biting into her bottom lip, eyes flooding with tears which she was unable to hold back. She wiped the back of a hand across her face irritably, poured hot water into an enamel bowl and added some disinfectant that made it go cloudy.

She tried to stifle the sob, but it was as much from frustration as upset. She worked jerkily, anger in every movement, slapped the hot water on to the wound and, ignoring his roar of startled pain, began to clean away the dried blood and accumulated dirt.

'Infection just starting to set in! How long have you been like this?'

'Few . . . days,' he gasped, trying to bite back against the pain. 'There was some trouble in—'

'I'm not interested!' she snapped rudely. 'I don't care how it happened. It's happened and it needs attention which I am now giving you – and make the most of it, Buck Enderby! Hate it or love it, it's the very last time you'll receive such attention from me!'

He twisted his drawn face towards her, puzzled.

'I'll dig out this bullet and I'll cleanse and treat the wound, but the next time you get shot, you go see a sawbones, or – or a damn Indian medicine man for all I care! Just don't bring your troubles back here! I've had enough.'

He moaned and groaned and grunted his way through the probing and removal of the bullet and sagged on to the kitchen table on his back where she had made him lay during the operation. She wadded clean cotton into the tunnel of the wound, made a pad to go over the outside and tore strips off a bed sheet to bind it in place. She helped him to his feet and headed him towards the tin hip-bath she had placed near the stove.

'Get undressed,' she ordered, as she took a pail outside and pumped water. He was sitting in the empty bath when she came back in and she snapped at him to get out. 'D'you want your bandages to get all wet? Just stand in it and I'll wash you down with wet cloths.'

'I'm not a child, damnit!' He almost fell and she steadied him.

'You sure act like one! You've never grown up. You turned up here seven or eight years ago wearing the rags of a Confederate uniform, covered in dirt under which I found three bullet wounds and two sabre cuts and a stone arrowhead. It seems to me I've spent the intervening years doing the same thing, over and over again!'

'And you've had a bellyful,' he said and gasped and rose to his toes as water sloshed over him.'God, that's cold!'

There was no more conversation until she had scrubbed and soaped him clean. She even dried him, brought him fresh clothes and helped him dress. As he sprawled in the chair, shaking and pale, she poured him some strong coffee, and filled the cup with whiskey. He sipped gratefully, holding the thick china cup in both hands.

'I'm mighty beholden to you, Kim. I'll never forget all you've done for me.'

'I hope you won't. But just remember, no more.'

'You're kicking me out?'

She sighed, taking a chair across the wet table from him, pouring herself some coffee. She busied herself with sugar and cream, stirring longer than was necessary, not looking at him as she spoke. 'It's been too long, Buck. You worked hard and helped me build up this ranch and for that I'm very grateful. Then you seemed to get some kind of wanderlust in you. Couldn't stay put more than a few weeks: once or twice you managed a few months but I saw what an effort it was for you. You always had some "job" or scheme that was going to make you a lot of money so you could put it into the ranch and really stock it up and buy more land, build a dam, *and I'm still waiting for it to happen!*'

He scratched at his head, pushing the damp hair back from his forehead. 'I always seemed to run into some unexpected trouble, Kim: lawmen, *crooked* lawmen, double-crossers, wrong information—'

'And the Enderby quick temper! Don't forget that, without it, you wouldn't have had a quarter of the "trouble" that's plagued and frustrated you. . . .'

He looked at her steadily now, a flintiness in his eyes. 'A man has to have his standards, my Pa told me that and I've tried to be like him. I won't be put-upon, or insulted or cheated by any man, or woman. If I have to settle things with my gun or fists, I'm ready to do that. . . .'

'More than ready, Buck, that's mostly your problem. You *like* trouble. You enjoy risks and fighting, but we don't have to go into all that. Just take note that from now on there is no haven for you here. You can ride out or stay and help me work the ranch, and we're doing pretty well. It's hard, but we're starting to show a profit and—'

'After all these years! You oughta be starting to show a profit, for God's sake!'

'You have to work for what you get in this life, I've always believed that.'

'Me too, you think I'm looking for some sort of easy ride? I risk my neck and I work damned hard on these chores I take on. I sell what talents I have, my muscles and my gun. . . .'

'And only once or twice have you come out ahead with a few dollars that aren't enough to buy a decent-sized herd! It's just not good enough, Buck!' She reached across the table and squeezed his hand. 'Oh, I know what chances you took to get those dollars, how hard it's been, the long recovery from your wounds. But did you stop to think of what I have to go through? Wondering where you are, especially when you don't turn up on time, whether you're even still alive. . . ?' Her voice was beginning to catch now and she felt herself tightening up with the effort but she didn't really care. This had been building up for a long time: it had to be said, should have been said long ago, but it was going to be said right *now!* 'Buck, I love you and I think you love me—'

'Well, I'm aiming to marry you, ain't I?'

She sighed again. 'So you say, but . . .'

He leaned forward, wincing, holding a hand over the wound, but his gaze not sliding away from her face. 'Why in hell you think I keep taking on these chores? Why do you think I'm chasing the fast money? Because I'm too blamed lazy to work for it? I'm greedy? Stupid?'

'Of course I don't think any of those things!' She snapped angrily.

'No, I guess I know that,' he said quietly. 'But if I'm gonna marry you, I ain't gonna do it while I'm poor. I grew up dirt-poor and hungry for sixteen years before that trouble with Asa Hunsecker and the Revenue men, and I was belly-growling hungry for another five years in the War after I lied about my age and joined the Army. But I didn't mind, because it saved my neck. I'm still a Tennessee renegade, daren't go back there, but then I ain't got anything to go back to anyway. First time I had a really full belly in my whole life, and could look forward to it each day, was after you took me in when the Reconstruction Vigilance Patrol chased me into them hills and I found my way down here. I've been here ever since except for this last year when I joined the Texas Rangers. . . .'

'The Rangers! And I thought you were dead all that time! Not a word from you! Until you turn up now with yet another bullet in you, your horse almost dying under you and—' She started to cry despite herself: it was something that rarely happened and it startled him. She released his hand, shook off his attempt to take hers back and dabbed at her eyes with a kerchief. She looked at him through tears, face twisted in anguish. 'You're a bastard, Buck Enderby! Putting me through that! And you've never even said you're sorry. . . .'

He squirmed. 'Hell, Kim, I was working down in Mexico most of the time. I speak Spanish pretty good so the Rangers used me for that reason, I didn't want to worry you. . . .'

'Worry!' She laughed shortly, coldly, without a trace of humour. 'It's a wonder my hair hasn't turned grey!' She paused and drew down a deep breath. 'But no more, Buck, *no more!* I mean it. You settle down on the ranch here, and prove to me you can do it, then we'll get married and – I pray to God! – live happily ever after. Now that's the deal I'm offering. If you're not interested, well, you can stay until you've recovered from this wound and then I'll help you pack your things and see you on your way.'

She was staring at him with defiance, a tremor in her voice, body rigid now, her kerchief in shreds, waiting for his answer.

'Let me sleep on it, huh?' he said wryly.

She threw the bowl of blood-stained antiseptic water into his face.

*

She served him breakfast in bed, obviously contrite. There was bacon, eggs from her chicken run, fresh-baked hot biscuits, corn fritters and freshly made coffee.

'Smells good,' he opined, sitting up, wincing at the pain the movement caused him.

She set the tray across his thighs, reached out and touched his tousled fair hair. 'I know you were just joking, I'm sorry I threw that filthy stuff all over you.'

He smiled crookedly. 'Guess I deserved it. Mmmm, this is good. Listen, I'm gonna work my butt off when this wound heals. I haven't done much around this place, used it mainly as somewhere to run to after I got myself into and out of trouble. You've a right to ask what you did and I'll do my best. If I don't measure up. . . .'

He shrugged and she leaned forward and kissed him, one hand stroking his stubbled face. Her eyes were moist and bright. 'I know I can be a bit of a harridan sometimes. But I would like you for a husband, Buck Enderby, we can be happy here. There's plenty of wilderness on our doorstep if you feel the urge to go primitive or something.' She paused, frowning a little. 'I know very little about you. I know there was some trouble back in Tennessee but you never went into details. You skim over everything to do with yourself. Why, it's not been long since you let slip that you used to be called "Bucky".'

He sipped some coffee. 'Well, I grew up called that. It was OK for a kid, but didn't seem to suit after a while in the army and I survived Gettysburg and so on.'

'There! I never even knew you fought at Gettysburg.' She was hard put to keep censure out of her voice.

'Nothing much to tell.'

'Why don't you let me be the judge of that?' She knew there was an edge to her words but she really was interested in his life. 'It's long past the time since we should've had such a talk, Buck, you know it is.'

Finally, he set down knife and fork on the cleaned platter, drained the coffee and reached for his tobacco sack and papers on the bedside table. She took them from him and rolled him a cigarette, lighting it and passing it across.

He drew in deeply and exhaled, composing his thoughts.

Tennessee seemed far away, and long ago. . . .

CHAPTER 2

LONG AGO AND FAR AWAY

Life was tough in the Big Smokies but it was a hell of a mighty fine place for a kid to grow up in.

The huge forests teemed with game and the occasional Indian, mostly Caddo, but sometimes wild renegade bucks from afar who would shoot anything that moved, including white men and women. There were skirmishes between them and the settlers but mostly life was just that, getting on with living and keeping enough food in your belly.

The Enderbys had been in Tennessee since way back when and no one knew when the first of them came to the Smokies. Family tradition had it that it was in the very early days of firearms development. Eventually one of them took to gunsmithing and made a name for himself as the finest maker of Kentucky hunting rifles anywhere on the continent, including even the Europeans at Lancaster.

Strangely, his talents weren't passed on to his descendants and although all the male Enderbys showed great interest in firearms, not one of them turned to the gunsmithing trade.

Mostly they used the knowledge in hunting, fighting Indians and the occasional outlaw gang that figured they could ride roughshod over the Tennesseeans.

And, later, for feuding with the Hunseckers.

Land and Cheatham Creek were the main points of contention. By this time moonshine had become the most lucrative and popular means of supporting a family, and Cheatham Creek had mighty fine runoff water with its source at a sweet spring high in the Smokies. Plenty of folk used it for moonshine but a section known as the Crystal Pools held the sweetest water of all, something to do with mineral content in the soil thereabouts.

It was partly on Hunsecker land, partly on Enderby holdings.

The Hunseckers were given to testing their moonshine output in large quantities, whereas the Enderbys were satisfied with a jug or two to keep out the cold and bodily 'knipshuns' (as Old Ma Enderby called any kind of illness way back, according to Pa). Drunk, and with their innate wildness and coarseness released, the Hunseckers were unpopular and feared in Nathan County, centre of the moonshine industry. They tried to take all of Crystal Pools for themselves and folk started to die on both sides. The feud went on for more than thirty years and then some kind of good sense seemed to prevail and the two families finally conceded there was more than enough Crystal Pool water for all of their needs.

They teamed-up when a bunch of Kentucky outlaws tried to move in and after that they lived side by side with only the occasional bust-out of hostilities that ended in quite serious injuries and, a couple of times, fatalities.

By this time, both the Hunsecker and Enderby patriarchs were growing old and their families had dwindled for different reasons, mostly illness and accidents. They tried to sort out any differences with fists rather than guns – except at the Turkey Shoots held regularly outside the town on Philmore Flats. Time after time the Enderbys won the prize – a twenty-dollar gold piece and however many turkeys they managed to shoot the eyes out of during the contest using Grandpa's old Kentucky rifle. Out of the blue one year, Cole Enderby faulted and missed his bird – Pa later accused him of thinking too much of that young Hunsecker girl they called Lucille – 'Lucky' Lucy, she was known as: lucky because she wasn't pregnant more times than she was the way she encouraged the young men of Nathan County.

No matter, that year the trophy was lost – to Asa Hunsecker, who vowed he would win every time from here on in.

Not the next time though. Jared beat him flat and Asa, deputy sheriff by this time, ambushed Jared afterwards and beat him badly. Just as he was crowing in his triumph, Pa Enderby came upon them and gave Asa the beating of his life. In fact, his life hung in the balance for some weeks afterwards and the Hunseckers began murmuring darkly about the renewal of the old feud.

But it didn't happen, at least not openly. There were a few fist fights between the Hunsecker boys and the Enderbys, including Bucky, but nothing too serious. Asa became sheriff eventually and he saw his chance to square things with Pa Enderby and get rid of some moonshine rivals at the same time. He called in the Revenue Men and led them to the Enderby still set-up in Hooty Owl Hollow.

Whether he knew he had picked two murderous sons of bitches or not was never made clear, but the Revenue Men figured here was a ready-made windfall, a set-up for the best moonshine this side of the Rockies, all for the taking. When Pa, Cole and Jared protested, the guns came out, Sheriff Hunsecker waiting in the trees and adding his shots to the battle started by the treacherous Revenuers.

Pa Enderby took Hunsecker's bullet in the head, Cole and Jared went down under the guns of the Revenue Men, and young Bucky Enderby, returning from a hunting trip, heard the shooting and arrived too late to save his family.

But he took his revenge with the Kentucky rifle and then lit out for places West. It was the only way to go. He was the last of the Enderbys and Nathan County was thick with Hunseckers. They came after him and he shot four of their horses and two of the men, fatally or not, he didn't know nor care.

By the time he had made his way out of the mountains and into Arkansas he heard there was war a'brewing. He tangled with two Hunseckers, laid an ambush and killed one, wounded the other, and made his way down into Mississippi. He arrived in Clarksdale in the midst of a brass-band-blaring, drum-thumping, firecracker spectacular that was a Recruiting Drive in disguise. Fearing there were still too many more Hunseckers on his trail yet, he changed his name to Bucky Nathan, put his age up by a couple of years and joined the newly-formed Mississippi Regiment.

He had always believed in Hell and after Gettysburg, Bull Run and The Wilderness, he knew exactly where Hell was, he'd been there and back. The others had called him loco and 'Crazy Buck' because of the way he ran to meet the enemy, into the face of their guns, his own weapons empty, only his bayonet to protect him.

'How come you act so crazy in a fight, Buck?' asked his troop sergeant one time while they sat, blood-soaked, wiping their bayonets, reloading, after a hellish charge. 'Way I see it, the idea is to shoot if you can, then duck or run so's you'll get home for Christmas!'

His blood-spattered face dead sober, Buck Enderby said, 'I don't have no home to go back to.'

And that was his only explanation and after a while they began to call him 'Lucky Buck'.

And, in fact, he *had* been unusually lucky, he came through the entire war with no more than a few superficial wounds. But it seemed that Fate had been saving him for something to correct the balance back in civilian life. He had always been a fine rifle shot and had demonstrated this skill a thousand times or more during the war, but afterwards, riding with a bunch of wild Texans set on returning to the Lone Star State as rich men, he had become more than proficient with a six-gun. He carried his gun in a soft leather holster riding high on his left hip, butt foremost – only later did he discover the more effiicent stiff-leather holster. But he was mighty fast on a cross-draw and had his first gunfight in a wildnerness camp one night with a bunch of bearded, broken-toothed killers who had made it clear they aimed to take everything Buck and his pards owned. No one called him 'Bucky' any longer, not after the big battles and seeing how he charged in amongst the Yankees with bayonet dripping blood, wild-eyed and unstoppable.

Two of the Texans he rode with were wounded from a fracas over a stagecoach hold-up north of Socorro and the third was ailing with fever. Buck Enderby seemed to be the only real stumbling block to the four killers and they wasted no time in bracing him.

He knew he was the only one who could stop them killing him and his companions. Maybe. So he figured why wait? Why waste time on talk when it was only going to end in gunsmoke anyway. . . ?

The biggest of the killer group spat into the fire, hoping to distract Buck while he reached for his gun, worn clumsily in a corner torn from a floursack on his right hip.

Buck Enderby's six-gun, a Remington Army in .44 calibre, simply appeared in his hand, flame stabbing out of the hexagonal muzzle, the hammer jumping as Enderby slapped at it again and again with the edge of his hand, the big gun bucking and roaring as it arced across the quartet of murderers and sent them to meet Old Nick.

The whole camp was shrouded in powdersmoke, the echoes of the shots rolling and slapping away through the woods. The fever-ridden Texan stared with bulging eyes. The other two wounded men struggled to sit up on their blankets.

'Judas priest, Buck!' breathed one, a man named Cord Brewster. 'That's the slickest damn thing I ever saw! Who showed you that trick with the hammer?'

Buck shrugged, already with his powder-flask and cast lead balls and percussion caps spread out on his worn blanket on the ground, preparing for the laborious business of reloading a cap-and-ball revolver.

'I just . . . did it. Figured, shooting normally, I might get two but by that time the others would have their guns out and a'smokin'. Didn't know if it would work but I've took enough guns apart and put 'em back together to figure it ought to be OK,' he shrugged casually. 'If it didn't, I was dead anyway, so what the hell?'

'Man, that was really something! You and me ought to make a good partnership one day.' Brewster grinned through the dirt and beard. It was a friendly grin, crinkled his eyes, the one that made the ladies feel all warm and quivery, usually knocked the edge off a man's anger – sometimes fatally for the one who thought he was getting out of trouble so easily. 'With my brains and your gun speed . . . hell, we can clean up, be rich men in no time.'

The others of their group looked at each other, a mite worried, but feeling a surge of anger deep down: what would happen to *them* if the two gunfighters teamed up? That was Cord Brewster's big failing, he was tactless, didn't care a damn about other folks' feelings—

Of course, it was inevitable that such a group, still smarting at what many saw as Lee's betrayal at Appomattox as forsaking the South, would run afoul of the Yankee Reconstruction.

They refused to knuckle under to the rigid, brutal laws enforced by the victors, made their own laws, and virtually took what they wanted. *To hell with Yankee Law in all its forms.* They held up payroll details, blew safes in Reconstruction headquarters, derailed trains, telling themselves they were still carrying on the Good Fight, South against the North. They became notorious, and there were several bounties on their heads. It was a wild life, not carefree, for they had to sleep with loaded guns under their pillows or in their hands. They had to steal most of their food and ammunition and certainly whatever money they needed. They rustled cattle, stole horses – from settlers and folk little better off than themselves, battlers against the wilderness and the Reconstruction that never showed any signs of going away, and now a new enemy, the scattered outlaw groups still loose and being hunted constantly by the Yankees.

It galled Buck Enderby and he said so in a mountain camp high in the sierras back of a place called Rafter Creek. What was really bothering him was the increasing abductions of young women from lonely settlers' cabins or occasionally from a stage they held up. Brewster and his friends used and then discarded them. Buck Enderby had known women while in the army, and afterwards, nearly all whores, but he had an innate respect for the opposite sex and finally, in that high camp at Rafter Creek when Brewster savagely slapped the current woman they were passing around, he snapped.

She had been taken from a cabin, home alone, claimed to be the young wife of a man who was somewhere in the hills looking for mavericks for their small holding. Tag Mitchell, one of the wild bunch, had shot a man he thought was trailing them in those hills above the cabin. It had occurred to Buck that it could well have been the young woman's husband.

That first stirred his compassion and then the way the gang had treated her – and he remembered all the others before her and knew there would be plenty yet to come – unless he did something about it. He had had enough and it was time to say so.

'Keep your hands to yourself, Cord!' he snapped and Brewster swung his head around, blinking, not believing he had heard right.

'What did you say?' He was genuinely puzzled.

Buck walked across and pulled the sobbing woman away from Brewster and then slapped him open-handed across the face, sending the big man staggering sideways. The others jumped to their feet but when Enderby looked at them, right hand hovering over his gun butt – the weapon now worn in a stiff-leather holster, greased on the inside – they backed off and made it clear they wanted no part of this. Whatever it might be.

The woman crouched, still sobbing, pathetically tugging the torn bodice of her dress in an attempt to cover her breasts, reddened and no doubt mighty sore from where Brewster and the others had been at her.

Brewster's eyes blazed and his handsome face, clean-shaven these days, was quickly turning decidedly ugly. He rubbed at his cheek and then the friendly smile crinkled his eyes once more. 'You son of a gun! You got religion, ain't you? Oh, I been watching, seen it coming, just wasn't quite ready for it. Hell! All them tales you told us about your Ma reading from the Bible, the only book you grew up with, I knew then you were gonna go soft sometime! Now it's happened.'

'Look, we're s'posed to be earning a living, outside the Law, sure, but that's just our way of thumbing our noses at the North and their goddamn Reconstruction, we ain't s'posed to be robbing our own kind, Southerners I mean.'

His hand flapped vaguely at the girl but Brewster scoffed. 'She ain't Southern, you blamed fool! She's Yankee trash! Moved in with her man and a carpetbag, aimin' to fleece us Texans and a—'

'She's only one of a couple of thousand Yankees. But never mind, I've had me a bellyful. I'm pulling out, and I'm taking her with me.'

Brewster's eyes narrowed. 'Pull out if you want, though I'll admit I'll be mighty sorry to lose a man so handy with a gun, but she stays! Till I'm good and through with her.'

Buck merely shook his head and waited. Brewster's face was hard. The others held their breath, to see these two squaring-off was *something!* Would it be guns or fists, they wondered. Either way it would be something to tell your kids about. Neither man would back down, they knew that.

Brewster spat, eyes narrowed now. 'She don't mean anythin' to you!'

'What's that got to do with it?'

Brewster laughed. 'God-*damn!* Knight in armour on a big white charger, huh? Man, you best leave that hillbilly upbringing way behind or you ain't gonna live much longer!'

'Long enough to do what I said.'

Brewster hesitated, then shook his head slowly. 'I don't think so.'

There was a collective sucking-in of breath from the others, including the wide-eyed young woman, as Buck's Remington appeared in his hand in a flash of blue-steel. He was already striding forward as he drew and Cord Brewster's gun was only halfway out of leather when the heavy Remington slammed him across the head and dropped him cold beside the woman who gave a small cry.

None of the others tried anything and Buck and the woman rode out, taking all the horses with them. He turned the mounts loose once they were out of the sierras and took the dishevelled, complaining woman within sight of the settlement at Rafter Creek. He had a few dollars and pressed them into her hand.

'Ma'am, don't look for your husband coming back – I don't think you'll ever see him again – I'm sorry for all that's happened to you. I hope you make out OK.'

She curled a split lip and he thought she was going to spit in his face but all she said, with savage hate, was: 'You Southern scum! We should have killed you all! Rid our world of vermin!'

He turned his mount and rode away, hearing her calling insults after him until he disappeared into the trees.

He hadn't travelled ten miles before he spotted the dustcloud behind him. The damn woman must've set the Reconstruction Vigilance Patrol on him, Enderby thought bitterly. *Well, he had sure stuck his neck out for that one!*

They were relentless and he rode two horses into the ground trying to outrun them. He stole a third mount from a corral and it was only half-broken and he had trouble fighting it along the trails. It delayed him long enough for the Vigilance Patrol to get within rifle shot and he had to make a stand. He nailed two of them but one got round behind and he took a bullet in the back. The Yankee whooped and jumped down from his boulder, running in to finish the job. Buck Enderby was hit bad but he had enough built-in fight left in him to draw the Remington and shoot the Yankee even as the man cocked the hammer on his rifle.

Enderby didn't recall much of how he got away from the rest of the patrol, but he found his way down out of the hills to an isolated ranch.

'Lucky it was your place, Kim.' Buck finished, reaching across to the bedside table for tobacco makings again. 'You took me in, sent the Vigilance Patrol away when they eventually came looking, stuffing me into your root cellar behind all them shelves of preserves. I owe you plenty, Kim, and it's about time I started to repay you.'

She nodded somewhat absently. 'You've had it rough, Buck. I'm glad you told me. But how come you went away this time and stayed away for so damn long?'

He looked uncomfortable, built and lit his cigarette before answering. 'Well, I got itchy feet like I had a few times before and told you I was going riding for a spell. Could see you didn't like it, but you never tried to stop me, seemed to savvy how I was, I liked that, still do. I came across a couple of hardcases who'd waylaid a man and woman on the trail, were tearing the clothes off her while the husband was on the ground, beat-up and unable to do much. He was trying but the one watching him just kept kicking him down, I needed a horse so I stepped in.'

'You . . . killed them both?' Kim asked, tightlipped.

'No choice . . . I gave the woman a blanket and started to patch up the man: he was a hell of a mess, face a mask of blood. But he said he was a doctor and would manage, said if I was ever in Del Rio to look him up – Bryce Franklin he said his name was.' Buck seemed far away for a moment. 'Somehow felt good. I knew I'd saved some decent folk this time, even if they were Yankees.'

He shrugged. 'I took the hardcases' horses and,

later, ran into some men in the hills, a Texas Ranger patrol. It was down near the Border and they were having trouble questioning some Mexicans about a gang of *contrabandistas.* I knew Spanish so I handled things for them and in the end they caught the smugglers red-handed. There was quite a gunfight and I got caught up in it. They said there might be a reward so I rode with them to Ranger Headquarters. Figured a few extra bucks would come in handy. I could start paying my way out here on your ranch, for one thing.'

Her face softened but he continued before she could speak. 'Think they kind of flimflammed me out of most of the reward, if there ever was one, but I didn't care, I was interested in the Rangers by then, the men having told me about 'em on the way back from the Border. They were keen to have me with them because I could use a gun pretty good as well as speak Spanish.'

He watched her face but it showed nothing much now.

'They said if I was interested in joining, I'd have to see their Captain Cordell . . . I figured I had nothing to lose by finding out a bit more, so they took me in to meet the Captain.' He paused again and looked steadily at her. 'It was Cord Brewster.'

CHAPTER 3

RANGER

Kim Preece looked sharply at Enderby as he made his announcement about Brewster.

'The same Brewster you gunwhipped for slapping that Yankee woman?'

He nodded. 'Called himself "Nathan" Cordell.' He smiled wryly. 'So he would never forget my name.'

'You hadn't told him your real name?'

'No – "Nathan" was what I used in the army, took it from my home County. It stuck afterwards but when I came here, one jump ahead of the Reconstruction Vigilance Patrol, I figured I might's well revert to "Enderby". No one knew me by that monicker outside of Tennessee.'

She nodded, watchful, as she asked, 'And how did Brewster greet you at Ranger Headquarters?'

'Sent the other Rangers out after they'd told him how I'd gotten involved, then gave me that old calculating stare and twisted smile I knew so damn well. . . .'

*

'Strange way for us to meet again, eh, Buck?' Brewster said from behind his desk, turning a pencil end-for-end in his big left hand. He moved his head a little so Enderby could see the left side of his face. There was a scar there that slightly pulled up the corner of his mouth. 'Put your brand on me with that Remington of yours, lost a couple of teeth, too.'

'Long time ago, Cord.'

Brewster stared hard and long, then, slowly, that old engaging smile widened. He slapped the pencil down hard against the desk, making a sharp, gunshot sound. 'Hell, yeah! You're right, we've both come a long ways, I reckon. You still on the drift?'

Buck said he was, just happened on the Rangers interrogating that Mexican.

'Still good in a gunfight, according to Brosnan. Can use a man like you.'

'In the Rangers? Brosnan said there might be a reward for the capture of those *contrabandistas.* That's really why I came.'

Brewster shrugged. 'Mexes might've had something out on him. We operate on a shoestring, no rewards, not even regular pay.' He gave Buck a sly look. 'But a mighty fine hiding place for a man on the dodge.'

Enderby grinned. 'So that's how come you joined up!' He indicated the wooden nameplate on the desk – *Captain Nathan Cordell.* 'You didn't waste any time.'

'Rangers had been disbanded by the Reconstruction and Governor Davis formed the State Police instead. He'd given 'em a licence to raise complete hell, no questions asked, but you know Texans. The State Police became a hot potato politically and about nine years after the war, a feller named L.H. McNeely from Washington County set up a new Ranger force. Even got 'em supplied with brand new Colt .45s, but the rifles were old Sharps buffalo guns till they decided to buy their own Winchesters. Dedicated men, at the time I was looking for somewhere to hide for a while, the Rangers were glad to grab anyone who knew which end of a gun was which. I had no trouble making "Captain Of Troop", not as fancy as it sounds. Still need good men, Buck. Pay's terrible, worktime's twenty-four hours a day and then some, but you get to smell gunsmoke and see places. And sometimes there's a bounty to be picked up.'

'Thought you were only s'posed to work in Texas?'

'That's the notion. But you get on the trail of some hardcase and he crosses a State Line or the Border.' He shrugged. 'Just carry your badge in your pocket instead of pinning it on your shirt and keep your head down, we get our man, even if we have to break a few laws to do it.'

Enderby was interested, he had this restless, unfulfilled feeling he couldn't shake. He had been happy enough at Kim's place but every so often the wanderlust had itched too bad to be scratched by just riding into town for a night in the saloons. He had to travel, put some distance under his feet. And – he admitted silently – he had that Enderby streak in him that seemed to need conflict every now and again. *Trouble-*

hunting, some called it. But his father used to say:

'There's a lot of enemies out there, boy. And once you've identified 'em, why wait for 'em to come to you? Go meet 'em and bury 'em, you'll sleep easier.'

So he joined the Rangers. Kim had taught him to read and write a little, and he signed 'Buck Enderby' on the application form before he realized it. Brewster smiled.

'So "Enderby's" the real name, huh?'

Buck cussed himself but it was too late now. 'Just like "Brewster's" yours.'

Brewster's smile faded. 'Yeah. Well, that's just between us. Hell, glad to have you with us, Buck. I can use that Spanish of yours. . . . You heard of Senator Pardoe?' When Buck shook his head, Brewster added, mouth twisted bitterly, 'Yankee, high up in the Reconstruction running the Lone Star State. Rich as all get-out, likely from carpet-bagging in the early days after the war, but he's a mighty powerful man. He helped get McNeely to form the Rangers again. Figures they're his baby, you know?'

Buck waited, having no idea where this was going.

'Got a boy – Renny – seventeen or thereabouts, spoiled rotten. Some woman trouble and one the Senator couldn't cover up easy so he sent the kid down to Mexico where he has some cattle holdings. Kid got into trouble down there, too. Messed with a *señorita*, youngest daughter of a *ranchero* named Diego, who was promised to some silver-haired old *hidalgo*, another powerful man, and he didn't like that gal bein' spoiled for him. Made it pretty damn hard and risky to try to get the kid back to the States so he's had to lay low. The men Pardoe sent down were good but not good enough, the kid's stuck down there in some rat-ridden village and Pardoe has been putting the pressure on me to use the Rangers to get him out. He'll pay a thousand bucks to the man who does it.'

Brewster stopped speaking, gave Enderby a quizzical look. Buck took his time, thinking how he could put that thousand dollars to good use.

'You'd have to go down as an ordinary cowpoke,' Brewster went on. 'Can't give you anything in the way of "official" assistance. But there'll be a few contacts, which is why your Spanish will be so handy.'

Buck made up his mind quickly: he owed Kim Preece plenty. He knew she didn't see it that way, but he had been brought up to always pay his way and this was a chance to do just that. Like it or not, he felt beholden to Kim and that thousand would help square things – in his mind, anyway. 'Better gimme the details, Cap'n.'

Brewster smiled in that friendly way of his, but Buck didn't notice the faint twist to the smile.

Maybe it was only from the scar left by the gunwhipping.

The village was in the Durango Region, called Gallatera. It was a known hang-out for men on the dodge, if they were headed south – most likely with US law breathing down their necks – they stopped for fresh mounts and grub. If they were headed north – maybe with Mexican law breathing fire on their tails – then they stopped to replenish supplies before the last long, dangerous run up to the Rio.

And there were others who more or less 'lived' there in Gallatera. They survived by preying on *norteamericanos*, whichever way they were going.

And there were those who, for a monetary consideration, would help these fugitives. At least, until the desperate men ran out of funds.

Then they were fair game, especially if there was a reward. If not, they would simply disappear from the face of the earth.

But Renny Pardoe was a special case.

He was being hidden from men who would drag him back to the old *hidalgo*, one Don Alvaro Balboa, for whatever reward he would pay. The men hiding Renny wanted money too, and would see that no harm came to the boy until they were sure they could take him back across the Rio and claim the thousand silver dollars offered by Senator Pardoe.

There were three hard-eyed, gun-hung Mexicans who watched over Renny Pardoe – Señors Ruiz, Mantello and Corzo. Each was a man feared in his trade and all of them had known the fearsome dungeons of the Region's notorious prison, Negra Sanctuario – Black Sanctuary. Some Mexican's idea of a joke, although legend had it that the prison was built on the site of an old monastery where the monks had dressed all in black, even to a mask over their faces, an outlawed sect that had fled Spain just ahead of the Inquisition's executioner.

The monks had offered sanctuary to any traveller, outlaw or pilgrim, but the monastery didn't last long.

Renny Pardoe's 'sanctuary' was in a cold, dirty adobe building on a rise just to the southwest of Gallatera's main plaza and the collection of shanties and crumbling houses that made up the village.

He was fed, lousy food by even a pig's standards, but better than nothing when you were starving. He wasn't really ill-treated – they shared an occasional whore with him – but it was no hotel. None of the three *caballeros* who guarded him took the least scrap of notice of his tantrums, content to wait until it was safe to move. Then another man arrived, said his name was Temprano, that he had received instructions from Renny's father to bring his son home safely at all costs – and the reward would be increased to two thousand silver dollars.

The bigger bounty interested the bodyguards, of course, but they did not see that they should share this with Temprano who showed no sign of moving out after delivering his message. He had the look of a gunfighter and deep down, they were afraid of him.

So they planned to murder him, using a whore to divert his attention, but held back because Temprano had hinted that he knew the plans for moving Renny Pardoe safely. Until the trio knew these plans, they couldn't kill Temprano. But word filtered from the town that men were gathering down there, *gringos* and Mexicans, who were planning on a concerted move against the sanctuary.

For, now, a counter-offer had been made by the Don Balboa – *five thousand pesos to the man who turned over the norteamericano violator of women to his men. . . .*

To Señors Ruiz, Mantello and Corzo, that sounded

like a better deal than two thousand American dollars.

But first, Temprano had to be eliminated and they began making plans to do this.

And into this hotbed of festering treachery and potential murder, rode Ranger Buck Enderby, carrying his badge pinned to his undershirt and his tuned Colt .45 in the greased and angled cross-draw holster.

It was a hot and sultry afternoon with threatening thunderheads blotting out the sun and bringing down early dusk to the Durango hillside.

He found his way out to the adobe on the rocky slope where Renny Pardoe was supposed to be guarded. His welcome was a rifle shot from behind some boulders and the bullet sang past his ear.

It was Ruiz who did the shooting, with an old Henry, and he levered in a fresh shell swiftly, intending to bring down the horse. But it looked a good one, a sturdy chestnut gelding, and Ruiz decided he could use such a fine mount. So he would shoot the man first. He shifted aim and stopped. . . .

Because the strange rider was no longer in the saddle.

Ruiz was bewildered, half stood to look into the small boulder field beside the trail. He did not notice that the Winchester '66 rifle was missing from the saddle scabbard, but he may have known an instant before Enderby's slug slammed into his chest and knocked him sprawling. Ruiz dropped the Henry, sobbing in pain, tasting blood. He fumbled at his revolver but by that time, Enderby was standing over him, the smoking muzzle of the rifle only inches from the Mexican's distorted face.

'You got Renny Pardoe inside?' Ruiz only gasped and spat blood. Enderby prodded him roughly with the rifle. 'You hear me, mister?'

Ruiz nodded, but his head was limp on his neck and his eyes were rolling up. Enderby knew he didn't need to waste another bullet on him. He threw the Henry and heavy old revolver into the boulders, got the chestnut under cover and made his way up the rest of the slope, dodging from rock to rock. He knew he was being watched from the adobe.

Twice bullets ricocheted from boulders an instant after he had passed them or thrown himself across. He didn't return the fire until he made the level ground where the tumbledown adobe stood. He saw the hardy mountain ponies in the corrals, settled in the rocks and fired.

One of the ponies dropped where it stood. Before it hit the ground, the one next to it reared up, pawing the air, shrilling, and then crashed on to its side, legs kicking feebly. A third joined the others.

'That only leaves two.' Enderby called, keeping his head well down. 'I can make it none, if you like!'

His answer was raking rifle fire, and the thunder of a shotgun. Nothing touched him. He left his hat jammed between two rocks and moved to his right, on his belly, using knees and elbows. He got out of line with the front windows and saw his hat spin away. Someone laughed in the shack.

Then he climbed up on to a high boulder, worked around until he was above the dry brush roof and jumped, aiming for a place three feet to the left of the chimney. He went in with splintering, rotten brush stalks collapsing under his weight. Dust choked and blinded him but he dropped flat on the earthen floor, rolled completely over and began shooting.

Before he had touched the floor he had seen the boy's form on a ragged bunk along one wall. That meant whoever moved on the floor was an enemy. They spun towards him, shocked.

His rifle was spitting flame and death as he worked lever and trigger and Señors Mantello and Corzo flung up their arms and crashed to the floor, Corzo jamming into a corner and managing to get off one more shot.

Buck Enderby nailed him with another bullet and felt lead burn across his arm, and again run like a drawn hot branding-iron down his left leg. It made his body jump but he twisted and flung the rifle at the shooter, the man crouched under a window. As he ducked, Enderby's right hand flashed across his body and there was a roaring Colt in his fist.

Temprano started to stand upright but the bullets beat him down and blood ran from a corner of his mouth. There was a brief bout of wracking coughing and he was still, his eyes open and staring blankly.

Enderby pushed upright, leaning his shoulders against the adobe wall, the smoking gun sweeping around and coming to rest pointing at the boy on the bunk.

He was filthy and dishevelled but even so, Buck saw that his dirty clothes had originally been of good quality.

'Renny Pardoe?' He examined his wounds but

figured they were only superficial. The kid was narrow-faced, smeared with grime. There was a slight fuzz on his jowls. His black hair was matted with dirt and, although he was leery of this man with the gun who had seemingly dropped out of the sky, there was still a tightness about his thin lips.

'Who . . . who're you?' The voice was a little shaky but still sounded demanding.

'Name's Buck Enderby. I'm a Texas Ranger, sent by your father.'

Renny stared, then jerked his head towards Temprano. '*He* said he was from the Senator. That the reward had been doubled.'

'Not true, kid. I'm here to take you back.'

'How do I know that? Did you bring me a change of clothes? A weapon? A note from my father. . . ?'

Enderby merely produced his badge and showed it to him. Renny Pardoe wasn't impressed.

'Hell, they sell them in the Plaza del Sol in Monterrey, for less than a peso.' His lip curled.

Enderby put the badge away, began gathering his things. 'You coming or not?'

Renny stared stubbornly, looking like he was going to throw a tantrum.

'That shooting will've been heard in the village. Someone'll be out here mighty soon. I'd just as leave not be here when they arrive. . . . You're walking money to those *peons*, kid.'

'Stop calling me "kid"! What if I don't want to come?'

Enderby glanced down at the dead men. 'Guess they won't be missed but does seem a waste of lead and powder if they didn't have to die right then. Well, you make up your mind, kid, Renny. I'm leaving. Pronto.'

He kicked open the rear door and started out. Renny hadn't made a move until the moment Enderby began running towards the boulders. At the same time there were shouts from the slope. He lifted on the bunk and saw, through the open window, a crowd of *peons* making their way towards the adobe shack. The first drops of rain spattered down.

'Wait! Wait up, damn you! I'm coming!'

Enderby didn't slow down, running from rock to rock, and the kid, afraid of the men now coming up the slope, followed, skidding and tumbling several times. Buck had made his way behind the corrals and he snatched a rope halter from the rails, slipped it over the head of a startled dappled pony, then kicked the rails loose and led the animal into the rocks. The men below started shooting.

Renny covered his head with his hands and sobbed in fear as he ran to where Enderby was now swinging into the saddle of his chestnut. He held out the rope on the pony as Renny staggered up, breathless. Rain drenched them both now.

'Get on.'

'There . . . there's no saddle!'

'You want one, go back for it – me, I'm moving out.'

Renny whined as Enderby dropped the halter rope and rowelled the chestnut, swinging it up the slope. Bullets kicked mud around the boy's feet and he gave a cry of alarm and flung himself across the pony's back, arms and head on one side, flailing legs on the other. The startled animal took off, and followed Enderby's chestnut up the slope.

Renny Pardoe kicked and cussed and actually cried in frustration but by the time they topped out on the crest and began to skid and slide down the other side, he had managed to struggle upright on the pony.

He groaned as the animal's bony ridge of spine pounded his buttocks. Rain lashed and lightning flared, both horses snorting and fighting the reins. But they made it out of town and into the hills and then through a series of dry washes, now half-flooded, into a narrow pass, and came out on the banks of a muddy creek. Enderby, allowing his chestnut a short drink, told Renny not to let the panting pony draw too much water into his belly.

'I don't take orders from you!'

Enderby slapped him. Not too hard, but a blow across the face that so startled the kid that he stumbled to one knee and his mouth sagged open as he stared up, wide-eyed at Buck. He rubbed his cheek which was reddening beneath the layer of grime. The rain had washed some of it off but there was still a stubborn, ingrained layer. 'You . . . you hit me!'

'And I'll do it again if you don't pay me mind, if you want to get out of here, you do what I say, and you do it pronto. Next time, I'll not only hit you, I'll leave you. I can use the reward, but I don't aim to get myself killed on account of a spoiled brat like you.'

Renny's thin chest was heaving wildly now. His mouth worked but he couldn't find enough breath to speak at first.

After they had crossed the creek and were riding through thorny brush, he snarled: 'Maybe I'll tell the Senator just how you treated me! See if you collect any reward then!'

Enderby didn't even look at him.

'You're a lousy bully!' the kid practically screamed. 'I'm only half your size and you . . . you think you can push me around.' There were tears of self-pity now, meandering through the remaining dirt on his face. 'The Senator'll fix you, mister!'

Enderby halted and Renny quickly wrenched his mount aside, blood draining from his face. He was obviously afraid Buck was going to hit him again, but Enderby turned and pointed to the distant grey line of the cordillera, showing in a flash of sizzling lightning.

'See that range? We've got to cross it by sundown tomorrow if we're going to have a fairly good run to the Rio. And the storm'll be over and there'll be plenty of mud for us to leave tracks in, so we'll ride all night.'

'I can't! Damn you! I need my rest! You've got a bedroll on your horse. Find us a cave and we'll rest up tonight. We can start early.'

'We ride, or you stay and I'll ride. Them's your options, kid.'

Pardoe's lips bunched up like a wrinkled strawberry. 'I'll never forget you, mister! *Never!* The Senator'll see to you, just you wait! We'll see who has the last laugh!'

CHAPTER 4

UNO MACHO HOMBRE

'And who did have the last laugh?' asked Kim when she brought in fresh coffee. They sat on the edge of the bed sipping from their cups, steam rising about their faces.

'Hard to say, the Senator seemed happy enough to get the kid back but Renny shrugged him off as quick as he could, threw me one more look that could've nailed me to the barn wall, and left the room. . . .'

'Afraid the boy's manners could do with improvement, Ranger.'

Senator Pardoe was a man in his fifties, enough steel grey at his temples and streaking his thick waves to give him a distinguished look. His face was a little flabby and his eyes could be disconcerting to some people, although they didn't bother Enderby.

'Having that chip on his shoulder likely helped him get through,' Buck said.

Pardoe frowned. 'You really think he has a chip on his shoulder?'

'Hell, yeah! 'Cause he's used to having his own way, that's obvious, and when he doesn't get it he thinks that throwing a tantrum will get it for him.'

The Senator watched Buck shrewdly. 'Didn't work with you though, did it?'

Enderby shrugged. 'Does this affect payment of the reward?'

Pardoe's face straightened. 'I see, strictly business, eh?'

Buck shrugged again. 'I need that money, Senator.'

'Well, you did a good job, Ranger and I won't forget it.' He stood, a tall man, but a little stooped. 'I may even use you again sometime. Come with me and you'll get your money.'

Kim frowned when Enderby paused and seemed as if he wasn't going to say any more.

'You haven't mentioned bringing home any money, as I recall,' she said tentatively. 'You've been away for just about a year . . .' She waited for some explanation.

He flicked his pale blue gaze to her face. 'No money, fact is, I was in jail for some of the time, and when I got out—'

'My God! You didn't mention that, either!' Her face tightened. 'You play your cards too damn close to your chest at times, Buck Enderby. . . !'

'Habit I've got, but it's saved my life on more'n one occasion—'

Kim drew in a deep breath. 'How did you end up in jail? I thought you were in the Rangers.'

'Was the Rangers put me there,' he told her with a crooked grin. . . .

The paper that Buck Enderby had signed was for a twelve month stint in the Texas Rangers and Brewster wouldn't allow him to just move on after finishing the Pardoe assignment so successfully.

'Hell, Buck, I'd be loco to let you go now! You did a helluva fine job, but one thing I've been meaning to ask: how did you know those three *caballeros* were gonna sell-out the kid?'

'Easy enough. They'd been in that adobe for some weeks, expenses paid by the Senator. Learned in a *cantina* in Gallatera that they had whores out there on a regular basis. Bought a couple of the ladies some drinks and they both mentioned the trio were planning to sell Renny to Don Balboa..'

'And Temprano?'

'Dunno, opportunist, I think. But he was trying to kill me, so I shot first, no questions asked.'

Brewster smiled crookedly. 'No wonder you were so damn good on patrol during the war. You always did get your preparation done well,' he sighed, shaking his head. 'But I still can't turn you loose, Buck. You signed on for one year minimum, with option for further service. You're stuck for another ten months.'

That didn't sit well with Enderby but he was philosophical about it. His next assignment was straightforward: clear up one of the rustling gangs on the Staked Plains.

Before he set off, he left his thousand dollars with

Brewster to put in the big office safe. He had never used a bank in his life, there were none in Nathan County simply because no one trusted them. A loose brick under the hearth was more in favour.

The rustlers gave him and his three companions a hell of a lot of trouble, including a long chase right down to the Rio. There was a running gunfight that ended in the Rio's muddy waters itself, all three of Buck's sidekicks down and nursing wounds. He swam the river, his rifle slung on a rope over his shoulders and climbed a tree. He picked off the four rustlers as they heaved their mounts up out of the water on the Mexican side.

A Mexican border patrol arrived and the *teniente* was mad as a hornet with smoke in its nest.

'A matter of jurisdiction, *señor,*' he insisted, a sour-faced man in his late thirties, with hard little eyes and a ragged black moustache. 'You and your Rangers show too little regard for our borders. I am under instruction to make an example out of the next *gringo* who violates our *frontera.*' He smiled without humour. 'Unfortunately, it seems to be you.'

'Turn your back for a minute, *teniente,* and when you look again, I'll be gone. Think of all that paper-work you'll save.'

The Lieutenant was offended. 'You think to bribe me, *gringo*! You think I am corruptible!'

Buck sighed. 'No – just look the other way. If I hadn't come across and nailed those bad *hombres* you'd have had four more *fugitivos* to deal with. Save everyone some trouble, just admire the scenery for a couple of minutes.'

But the *teniente* was furious and shouted and reached for his sabre. Buck didn't waste any more time. He brought the butt of his Winchester around quickly, and sent the lieutenant hurtling from the saddle into the shallows, now stained with the dead rustlers' blood. Buck swung back, the rifle shooting over the heads of the six-man patrol. The Mexicans froze, slow to react because of the shock of seeing their officer knocked out of the saddle. Slowly, they raised their hands shoulder high. Buck made them toss their weapons way out into the river.

Then he jerked his head to the *teniente* who was lying face down in the river. 'Best get him out of there.' When they obeyed, and while they dragged their officer up the bank, he fired several shots under their mounts' feet, grabbed one's bridle, swung into the saddle and swam it back across the Rio to where his wounded companions waited.

'Judas,' said Buddy Brosnan nursing a bloody shoulder. 'You've sure done it now, Buck! That lieutenant gets pissed at you – and I can't see why he wouldn't – we could have an international incident on our hands.'

Brosnan was right and Brewster fumed and stormed about his office as he cussed-out Buck Enderby.

'You goddamn hillbilly! You can't go trespassing over to Mexico whenever you like and then gunwhip one of their border patrol!' As he said 'gunwhip' his left hand involuntarily touched the deep scar on his own face. His eyes clouded. 'Seem to have a fancy for gunwhipping, don't you?'

Enderby was a little surprised at the amount of hatred Brewster let show, wondering just how much he had been supressing while he had been acting 'friendly'.

Brewster shook his head. 'God almighty, Buck! This isn't going to blow over. It's gonna be official and you could be in a lot of trouble—'

'I'm no stranger to that, hell, Cord, I nailed the rustlers, got all my pards back alive. Rangers ought to back me.'

Brewster sat down, fingers tapping one arm of his chair as he frowned. 'Ye-ah, they might. But they won't risk any kind of a political situation that'll make the Mexes mad enough to take it to Washington.'

That jarred Buck. 'Washington!'

'Hell, yeah! We've been in a fair bit of trouble lately, violating their sovereignty as they call it. They want to be taken seriously as a nation and they're mighty touchy. You lay low for a spell. I'll put you on some chores around here, helping the wrangler, or something, but I'm gonna have to take this higher.'

Enderby enjoyed breaking in horses and helping the wrangler to catch mustangs up in the hills. A couple of weeks passed and he figured the trouble with the *teniente* had blown over. He was wrong, it had just been decided.

And he didn't like the decision at all.

'Looks like you're a scapegoat, Buck, old pard,' Brewster told him after calling him to his office. He didn't sound too concerned about the obvious bad news he was about to impart. 'The Mexes will back off, providing we discipline you.'

'Which means—?' Enderby asked warily.

He was sure Brewster covered a crooked smile as he shuffled some papers and said, 'Looks like you'll do six months in San Antonio Stockade. . . .'

Enderby couldn't believe it. He didn't know what he had been expecting but it sure wasn't that.

Brewster rang his handbell on his desk as he finished speaking and two Rangers entered, carrying carbines, not meeting Buck's eyes.

'Turn him over to the escort,' Brewster said, signing something, folding the paper, and slipping it into a long brown envelope which he sealed and handed to the closest Ranger. It was Buddy Brosnan and as he reached past Enderby to take the envelope he murmured,

'Sorry, Buck.'

As they started out, Enderby, disarmed now and walking between the other two, Brewster said, 'Don't worry about your guns, or your money, Buck. We'll keep 'em safe for you.'

Buck Enderby had never been confined for more than a day in his life. Sheriff Asa Hunsecker had hauled him in with his brothers one time and had tried to coerce him into admitting that the Enderbys had a still hidden somewhere on their property. When that failed, Hunsecker had turned nasty and tried threats but pulled up short of physical violence. He gave up and turned Buck loose that afternoon, though he had kept Cole and Jared for a couple of days, claiming they had caused some damage in a brawl at the saloon.

Confined spaces – when there was no possibility of a way out – bothered Buck Enderby. The jail wasn't all that bad, he admitted, they worked the quarry or on roads with a chain gang, felled timber for railroad ties and rough-sawn planks for ranch buildings, all in the open air. But it was night time when he was chained to a communal iron bar running the length of the hard pine platform where the prisoners slept side by side, with barely room to turn over, that bothered him most. It was no fun with the anklets on: a man had to kind of twist his feet and cramps added to the discomfort. The cuffs rubbed skin raw, too, which stung with perspiration or became infected from working ankle deep in mud in the thickets.

He fought down the rising panic in him each night, felt his belly beginning to tighten at the thought of that confinement after the slops they were fed for supper each day.

At the end of the first month he had learned to live with the situation, figuring he was only making things worse by trying to fight something he couldn't beat.

Then that thought stirred him; why not look upon it as a challenge? Give him something to think about apart from all the discomfort and pain of serving time.

Armed guards were everywhere. The fact he was a Ranger meant nothing to them, he was a convict, and treated the same as the others, perhaps a mite more harshly. There were rough men in that jail who had no use for a Ranger in any shape or form. Two had tried to stab him and he hadn't been ready, the home made blade had sliced his ribs and chest but a guard had been sighted and the men had hurried away. He hid his wounds and made no complaint.

But he caught one of those men in the thicket some time later. They said afterward it looked as if the man had been savaged by a wolf or a cougar. He was so smashed-up he spent three months in the infirmary. The other man who had tried to stab Enderby made his peace.

One other tried to start a fight, no doubt with his cronies in the crowd waiting to step in in the confusion and kill or maim Buck.

But he was alert for trouble and had worked at loosening the head on his pickaxe. When the giant bully had moved in, Buck slipped the head off the hickory handle, spun around and rammed the end into the man's belly. When the stinking breath had gusted out and the large man had doubled up, he laid the handle alongside the man's ear and stretched him out, mouth shattered, nose spread all over his face. He slipped the pickaxe head back on the handle and continued his work.

He never knew what the bully's friends had told the guards when they found him bleeding and unconscious, but one of them, a Mexican, when helping roll a big boulder across to the crushing detail, said, 'You are *uno macho hombre, señor!* My felicitations!'

One hard man . . . well, Buck reckoned that was just what you needed to be if you aimed to survive in this place.

Survival was his aim, but not in here. He had had a bellyful and he was ready to leave.

There were armed guards every few yards it seemed when the inmates were working on the chain gang, felling trees or clearing brush for the roads, or doing any work outside the prison walls. Two men during Buck's stay had made attempts to escape.

The first had asked permission to go to the water-butt for a drink, obtained it, but instead, tipped over the barrel on the slope. It was high up, not just so it could be seen by the guards from their stations, but also to make the convicts work for their drink. Fifty gallons of water swept the feet out from under the guard and while he was still floundering, the prisoner jumped on him, grabbed his rifle and ran.

He stopped to trade lead with the other guards and that was his undoing. If he had just kept running into the brush he might have made it – might have – stopping to shoot back was his big mistake. For one thing, it gave them a stationary target and six bullets blew him to rags and hurled his body a yard or two into the gully. . . .

The second man didn't seem to care whether he made it or not, the way he acted Buck suspected that getting himself killed was his *sure* way of escape.

He tried to strangle the guard near the gear wagon, threw the half-choked man from him, leapt into the seat and tried to whip up the team. The wagon had only creaked about five yards before he was blown out of the seat. . . .

'Plumb loco tryin' anythin', with all them guards

and guns around,' was the general opinion. 'Just gotta get used to it, *compadres.* We is here to stay, we serve our time and *then* we gets out. Or else we dies and gets out earlier!' Jail humour, thought Enderby but gave the matter some thought and figured he might just be able to pull off his escape.

He said nothing to anybody, waited until a guard named Shaw was on lock-down duty at night. No guard wore a gun in the barracks. An armed man stood guard outside the locked door, while the duty man walked down the line, clamping the anklets around each man, who was supposed to have his feet ready and resting on the iron bar.

Except this night Buck Enderby's feet were on the planks inside the bar line. Shaw rapped his ankle hard with the iron cuff. Buck moaned but didn't move his feet.

'The hell's wrong with you, mister?' barked Shaw.

'Guess he's plumb tuckered, sir,' said the man next in line, no real friend of Buck's but not wanting any trouble this close to himself.

'Well now, ain't that a shame . . . guess I'll just have to wake him up!' Shaw grinned, baring chipped teeth, eyes bright as he lifted the iron cuff and prepared to really smash it across Buck's ankles. Instead, Enderby's leather-soled foot – they did not wear boots on work details – smashed the words back into his throat.

A low gasp ran through the barracks but even in their shock, the prisoners didn't make it loud enough for the man outside the door to hear. Buck was already moving, uncoiling off the sleeping planks, hurling himself bodily at Shaw. His weight carried him over and down to the flagged floor. Buck snatched the chain and iron cuff from the guard's hands and slammed him twice savagely across the skull. Shaw went limp and before all the breath had gone out of him, Enderby was unbuttoning the man's tunic.

The prisoners were excited, urging him on in hushed encouragement. He stripped Shaw swiftly, had chosen him because he was about Buck's own build, dressed as fast as he could and pulled on the boots without socks. They hurt his swollen feet but he gritted his teeth, grabbed the man's cap and jammed it low over his eyes, shoving his long, filthy hair up beneath the cloth. Carrying the big key ring, he gave a mocking wave to the others and hurried towards the door. He knocked on the door, the inmates now holding their breath, waiting to see if he would get away with this totally insane attempt at escape.

The unsuspecting guard outside unlocked the door and pushed it inwards, his rifle held loosely in one hand. His face registered incredulity as he belatedly recognized Buck Enderby. By then the iron cuff on its chain was whistling towards his head, connected, and he collapsed.

Enderby snatched the rifle, buckled on the pistol belt and holster. He flung the guard inside, tossed the keys on to the sleeping planks, then closed the door, locking it. He didn't think the others would try anything, it would be too risky moving about the prison in their convict rags.

Whereas he, in guards' uniform, obviously armed,

could go almost anywhere he liked. Which included the tool shed. He had left a hard piece of granite behind a bigger rock near the door. It took only three blows to break the hasp on the padlock.

He took a coil of rope used for hauling logs, complete with hooks to drive into the wood. It took him seven throws before that hook, padded now with rags torn from an old coat hanging up, caught on the edge of the wall, on a part out of sight of the main guards.

He was thin and malnourished, but the hard labour had kept his strength high. He went over in a couple of minutes, lowered the rope, slid down into darkness and breathed free fresh air for the first time in more than three months.

CHAPTER 5

FREE!

Buddy Brosnan, now a sergeant in the Rangers, knocked on Brewster's office door and waited for the Captain to call out that he could enter.

Brewster was sitting behind his desk, cluttered to look as if he was up to his eyebrows in work, though this was not necessarily so. Cord Brewster wasn't a man who believed in busting a gut for a dollar – which was one reason he had joined the Rangers and called in favours and stabbed a few backs to become a Captain of Troop working out of San Angelo.

He set down the pen and eased back in his chair as he saw who had entered. 'What is it, Bud?'

Brosnan, putting on weight since he had become sergeant and had more money to spend on carousing, eased back his hat and, wheezing a little, jerked a thumb over his shoulder.

'That Mex is back again, sittin' by the flagpole, Cap.' He knew better than to call Brewster 'Cord' as the man's first name had now become his surname for the benefit of the Rangers.

'What Mex?' There was irritation in Brewster's voice: he had little use for the US's neighbours below the Rio.

'The one that's been hangin' around for nigh on two days, I told you yesterday. Says he wants to see you.'

'Yeah? Well, kick his ass out of it. I don't want to see him or any other greaser for the matter of that.'

Brosnan sniffed, somehow making the tip of his nose slew and twist, wiped the back of a wrist across his nostrils and cleared his throat. 'Says he'll shoot any *gringo* who tries to move him before he talks to you. Reckons whatever it is is mighty important.'

'*He* reckons, huh?' Brewster's mouth was grim, no sign of the friendly smile now. 'Well, tell you what, you go and kick his ass off the station like I told you!'

'He's nursin' a big old Colt Dragoon!'

'Judas priest, how many men we got here?'

'Most are away on duty, Cap—'

'How many men?' Brewster roared and Brosnan did some hurried calculations, came up with four, five counting himself. 'Well, you count yourself and get rid of that Mex! Now!'

Brosnan nodded and hurried out and Brewster leaned back in his chair again, groped for a cigarillo and lit up. He went to the window to look out into the yard. Brosnan was leading four Rangers over to where, sure enough, there was a serape-clad Mexican sitting with his back against the flagpole next to the stacked cannon balls beside the old wheeled cannon that had seen action on a dozen battlefields during the War.

When he was still several yards away, Brosnan began yelling at the Mexican, the others shambling along, no doubt annoyed that they had been interrupted in whatever they were doing. The Mexican stood, moving quickly for a greaser, Brewster thought, tall, too. His hand went beneath his serape as Brosnan reached him and two of the others moved around to get behind. But the man, now holding a large old Colt Dragoon, which weighed over four pounds, began swinging the gun in a wide arc, backed up. The Rangers jumped back, the boredom suddenly dropping from their faces as they realized this fool was prepared to fight them.

Still – five to one! The man must be loco!

It wasn't enough.

Brosnan went down first, hugging ribs that creaked and sent slivers of razor-sharp pain through his side as the Dragoon cracked him. A Ranger trooper closing in fast, staggered as the serape suddenly coiled around his face and head, blinding him. He staggered into the pole and the Mexican, now revealed as being dressed in ragged range clothes, slammed his head hard into the wood. A third man walked into a fist between the eyes and stumbled over the man sagging at the foot of the flagpole. The fourth and fifth men, wishing they had worn their guns, moved in more warily.

The Mexican, still backing off, reached the pyramid of cannon balls, scooped one up in his left hand – no mean feat when each one weighed at least seven pounds – and rolled it towards the men. They danced and dodged, not wanting crushed feet, and the Mexican banged their heads together. Groaning, they fell to their knees.

Standing amongst the moaning, scattered Rangers the man turned towards the building and Brewster, looking astonished at his window. The Mexican pushed back his straw, ragged-edge sombrero, revealing a dark, gaunt face, just a glimpse, before he pulled down the hat again.

Brewster had seen, though, and recognized the man. He opened the window and called, 'Come on up, *amigo*! Reckon you've earned it!'

He was seated behind his desk with a bottle of whiskey and two shotglasses before him when the Mexican came in, wearing his serape again now, and closed the door behind him.

'You son of a bitch!' Brewster said with the old smile. 'Why the hell didn't you say who you were? You know I don't care for greasers.'

As he dropped into a chair, Buck Enderby tossed the old straw hat to the floor and shrugged, draping the serape over the back. 'Figured you'd have some kind of dodger on me on your desk. Didn't want your men to try and collect any reward.'

Brewster laughed, shaking his head as he poured two drinks, pushing one slopping glass across to Enderby who tossed it down quickly.

'Needed that, huh?' Brewster said, still grinning, and tossing down his own whiskey. He poured two more and sat back, nursing the glass, studying him. 'You sure lost weight in that jail. Makes you look meaner.'

'Not the place to sweeten your disposition.'

'Guess not. Well, you can relax. No Wanted notice out on you.' Enderby arched his eyebrows, paused with his glass halfway to his mouth. Brewster's smile took on a twist. 'You've got the luck of the Irish or something, *amigo.* Your timing was just about perfect. You busted out just as the powers-that-be, thanks to some wrangling and pressure brought on 'em mainly by Senator Pardoe, decided that you serving three-and-a-half months was enough to keep the Mex Government happy and satisfied that you'd been disciplined for trespassing and knocking down that lieutenant.'

'What's that mean?'

Brewster spread his arms. 'Means, they decided to parole you. It would've been through in a few more days, anyway.'

'I don't believe it . . . I've never had anything that easy in my life.'

'Well, rub your Rosary or your lucky rabbit's foot or something, but that's how it stands.' He picked up a paper from his desk, handed it across. 'Official notification, 'course you busted out before the parole came through and nobody liked that, but Pardoe had his way and pushed for the parole. The guards you knocked out mightn't be too happy but they'll do what they're told—'

Buck handed the paper back. He could only read some of the words anyway but he saw the seal of the New Texas Government and that was good enough for him. 'You're sure?'

Brewster scowled at the paper a little, then brightened his face as he set it down on his desk. 'Pretty much. You got friends in high places now. Pardoe's taken a shine to you. Seems his kid kinda likes you, too.'

Enderby scoffed. 'After the way I dragged him back? He must be putting on an act for the old man or something.'

'Whatever, it worked for you.'

Enderby was silent and Brewster watched him closely, asked suddenly, 'What made you take a chance and come here anyway? I mean, you didn't know any parole was coming.'

Buck looked him straight in the eye. 'I came for my thousand bucks.'

Brewster nodded slowly. 'Thought that might be it. Needed it for your getaway, huh?'

'*Still* need it.' No one knew about Kim Preece and Buck aimed to make sure no ever got to know about his connection with her. He had missed her and the mostly boring ranch life far more than he would have thought possible while in jail, of course, *anything* was better than being in that hell-hole, but he figured when he got out, he would quit the Rangers, take that thousand from the Senator and go on back to Kim's place, and this time settle down for keeps. Sure, it would take a heap of doing, but now he knew just what he was missing and he was all set to give it his best shot.

He noticed that Brewster was turning a pencil end-for-end between his fingers again, a sure sign of his irritation. He looked mighty sober.

'What's wrong, Cord?'

'Don't use that name here, damnit!' Brewster snapped, but Buck had a notion the man was just using it as an excuse to stall a little longer. 'Your money, Buck . . . we had a robbery not long after you went to San Antonio—'

'Robbery!'

'Yeah . . . right here.'

'Why the hell would anyone bust into a Texas Rangers office?'

'You might be surprised, it's happened in other stations and law offices, sometimes they're after guns, because there're always racks of 'em in such places. Sometimes it's just to mess up the place, someone being vindictive because of the way they been treated, and sometimes it's money. Lots of law offices carry cash to pay out on bounties—'

'Well. Guess I never knew that,' Enderby said very slowly, still looking hard at Brewster. 'Never heard of it before, matter of fact—'

'Oh, yeah, fairly common, this one happened when we was snowed under with work, had the whole troop scattered all over the southwest. Was just me, the cook and an orderly that particular night.' He half-turned in the chair and indicated the big green safe. 'Cleaned it out, took some official papers, which our investigations made us think was maybe the real reason for the bust-in, but no one would pass up that amount of money, I reckon.'

Enderby stood and examined the safe. 'Seems pretty much secure to me. You never heard a thing?'

Brewster shook his head. 'Cook was drunk, orderly was home with his wife, and I was, well, kind of occupied with a certain lady in town, a certain *married* lady.'

Enderby stared and then nodded gently, returning to his chair. 'How much was in there?'

'Apart from your thousand? Aw, some petty cash, little over two hundred . . . pretty good haul for whoever did it.'

'No clues?'

'Only that we think it might've been something to do with disbanding the Rangers, which is why the books were stolen. Lot of people don't like us, you know.'

'Found that out in jail. Well, looks like no chance of recovery, huh?'

Brewster was very sober now. He picked up the pencil again – *tap, tap, tap* – as he rotated it end-for-end. He shook his head. 'Sorry, Buck, sorry as all get-out. I busted my ass trying to find who it was, knew you'd need that money when you were released. I reckon it's gone for keeps.'

'Yeah, so do I.' There was bitterness in Enderby and he let it show. *To hell with Cord Brewster, the lying son of a bitch!* 'Well, what happens now? Am I free to go?'

'Well, guess I'll have to keep you around until the official parole is fixed, but you'll have to serve out the rest of your time in the Rangers, too—'

'Hell, I figured you'd be able to fix something to get me out of that.'

Brewster was suspicious of the way Buck said it, was he inferring something? That maybe he would like to get rid of Buck out of the Rangers right now?

'Listen, Pardoe's behind you in this. Why, it's his business, he's fixed it for you to be released into his custody. You'll be on his ranch outside of Painted Rock in Concho County for the next three months and I know damn well if that's what Pardoe wants, it's what he'll get. He'll fix it somehow, no idea what he wants with you, but I've gotta keep on the right side of the Senator. Could make it an assignment, I suppose, your last one in the Rangers, although you'll still have time to serve after the parole. Take some juggling, but you've had some bad luck and a raw deal, Buck, and we were pards for a long time. Least I can do I reckon. Interested?'

Enderby sighed. 'Well, I don't much like the sound of what Pardoe's got in mind, seems to me he wants me to nursemaid that damn kid, but if it has to be, I guess it has to be. Better than that jail, anyway.'

Brewster smiled the warm smile, stood up and offered his hand. Buck took it after a few seconds. Their eyes met across the desk.

'I'll look after things, Buck. Meantime, you're confined to these here barracks, just till the parole becomes official, so just take it easy for now. I'll get a sawbones in to take a look at you, and Cooky can whip up some decent grub, sound OK?'

Enderby nodded, still looking into Brewster's smiling face. 'Sounds good, about a thousand bucks' worth of consideration, I'd reckon. . . .'

The smile faded slowly from Brewster's face.

Buck Enderby was not really surprised to find the Senator himself waiting at the ranch in the hills behind Painted Rock. Pardoe looked upon it as a 'small' holding, but it was one of the biggest spreads Buck had seen.

And it suited him, he needed some wide open spaces for a while, give him a chance to shake off that damn claustrophobic feeling left over from the jail.

The Senator's welcome was effusive but Buck figured much of it was put on, the man seemed restless, impatient with just about everything and everyone. He led the way into a small room obviously used as the ranch office. As well as a desk and a wooden filing cabinet and stacks of old newspapers and back-east magazines scattered around, there was saddle gear and some spare workclothes, torn ponchos and old boots, likely abandoned by men long departed from the ranch, now available for any of the hands who were in need of such things. The spread was called the R Bar P, which Enderby correctly surmised was meant to be 'Renny Pardoe' with the bar linking the initials.

It looked like the spread was going to belong to the kid one day, could be the Senator had set it up in an effort to bring Renny to heel, get him to stick around, show some real responsibility. But those things were really the father's job, Buck thought, and no ranch or anything else could do it for the parent.

But *he* was going to have to try.

The Senator got right down to tin-tacks and told him the kid had spoken with something like affection about Enderby and he thought it would do Renny good to have a few months under Buck's guidance.

'Still got something like six months or more for your term in the Rangers, Buck, three of which at least you'll spend here, see what you can do with him.'

Enderby was uncomfortable. 'You sure the kid'll go along with that arrangement?'

The Senator's mouth tightened. 'He will! Or I'll know the reason why—'

'Well, there's a problem right at the start. If Renny's not willing to make a try at pulling himself together, I'm not going to get very far. He's likely to tell me to go to hell and light out for the hills.'

Pardoe banged a fist down on the edge of the desk, shoulders hunching as he leaned forward. '*No!* There'll be none of that. You'll be in charge and he'll obey, or he'll answer to me.' He quietened down abruptly and said, 'Look, you brought him home safely from Mexico and however you did it, it made an impression on him. He might not admit it but it's true. Just use the same kind of thing now.'

Buck smiled thinly. 'I was looking after my own hide then, too, and I couldn't afford any tantrums that might've gotten us both killed. I was a little rough at times.'

Pardoe's mouth tightened again but he nodded resignedly and flapped a hand. 'OK, I've thought maybe I should have been a bit . . . rougher with him, too, but truth is, Buck, I was too involved with my career and I left it to whoever was handy to bring him up. I'm paying for that neglect of him now and I can savvy how he feels. But you straighten him out and I reckon he'll come around.'

Enderby didn't want any part of this, but he knew he was beholden to Senator Pardoe, being instrumental in getting him the parole, and he felt mighty uncomfortable about his lack of enthusiasm. 'You ever tried it before? Had someone else take him in hand?'

'Sure, got a man with him now, Lane Magill. Seemed OK, decent type, worked on my big ranch. Sent him down here to take Renny in hand—' He shook his head. 'Didn't work. He'll be fired. Now I'm putting my faith in you, Buck.'

'Why the hell you think I can do anything? I was youngest of five kids. The others brought me up. I dunno anything about bringing up kids like Renny—'

'A spoiled brat, you mean? Thing is, Buck, you people in the Smokies, Tennesseeans, Kentuckians – well, we call you hillbillies, but I've toured those places, with the Reconstruction right after the war. I've seen families and how they act. You folk might not be too worldly, but you seem to know how to bring out the best in other human beings, 'specially kin, show respect for their elders and so on.'

He paused, looking embarrassed. 'Guess I sound kind of stupid, but fact is, Buck, if I go on to become Governor here, and that's my ultimate ambition, then folk are more likely to vote for me if they see I have the support of my own son. Wife's long dead, daughter's up north in our home State of Pennsylvania, respectably married with a growing family, but too far away to really do my career a lot of good.' He frowned, looking at Buck Enderby now. 'What's wrong?'

'You're doing this for Renny or your career?'

Pardoe actually flushed. 'Well, both, damnit! I

want a son to back me, stand at my side, show his respect for me in public, but I want it for him too! I want him to be a decent kind of human being.' Suddenly, he seemed to realize he was baring his soul too much, pulled the parole notice across to him abruptly and reached for a pen, dipping it into the glass well. 'Now, you want to help me out or not?'

The pen poised above the space that needed the Senator's signature to make the parole official.

Enderby figured he had done some mighty foolish things during his life, but he wasn't that big a fool that he would refuse to take on this chore. Even if it killed him.

And it damn near did.

CHAPTER 6

WALK TALL

Lane Magill met Enderby when he rode out to the line camp above the main ranch, on a grassy bench halfway up the mountain.

He was a tall man, muscle-padded, with suspicious eyes and a hard face. He was also a man with a gun.

The rifle he held was cocked and he had a finger already resting on the trigger guard as he stepped down from the line shack's stoop to the uneven ground and watched Buck dismount lazily at the pole corral which held a half-dozen horses as a small remuda.

'You got a name, stranger?' Magill called.

'Buck Enderby.'

Magill nodded, and the rifle swung down and around, casually pointing at the newcomer. 'Here to see the kid, huh?'

Buck walked up slowly, tugging on his work gloves. He had picked up a proper curl-brimmed hat at the

R-Bar-P house and he carried the big cap-and-ball Dragoon pistol rammed into his belt. 'Mind not pointing that gun at me?'

'Yeah, I mind, I ain't about to make you welcome, Enderby. You're takin' over my job . . . I heard all about you and the Senator arrangin' for your parole.'

'Then you know it's Renny I came to see, not you. So, one more time, point the gun somewhere else.'

Magill bared his teeth, tightening his grip on the rifle. 'Say "please".'

Buck sighed, looked down to tug his left glove tighter, and then his right hand blurred the few extra inches to the Dragoon and the mountainside shook to the thunder of the big powder charge. Lane Magill yelped and jumped back both hands tingling as the heavy ball tore the rifle from his grip.

'Judas priest!' he gasped, eyes widening. He looked down at the Winchester which had come to rest against one of the wooden stumps under a corner of the shack. The action's brass cover plate was mangled and heavily dented, the lever jammed partly open. 'You bust my gun!'

'Should've busted your head. Where's Renny?'

Magill tightened his mouth childishly, eyes blazing as he rubbed his hands. Then Buck heard the clatter of hoofs up-slope and he flicked his gaze there, seeing Renny Pardoe work his horse deftly down the slope through the timber. The kid rode in, hauling rein, taking in the situation swiftly. He gave a crooked smile and dismounted, walking across to stand between Magill and Enderby, looking at the latter.

'Might've known you'd arrived. Still throwing your weight around, I see.'

Enderby nodded gently and looked steadily at Magill who was scowling and angry. 'The Senator said to send you on down and you can draw your time.'

'I don't take orders from you!' Magill looked hard at Renny. 'You really want this son of a bitch to take over? Wipin' your nose for you, runnin' your errands, pickin' up after you?' The hard eyes swung to Enderby, mocking. ' 'Cause that's what you'll be doin', hillbilly. This here is the champeen spoiled brat of the whole blamed southwest.'

'That's about to change,' Buck said easily and ignored the tightening of Renny's face and the narrowing of his eyes as the kid straightened. He started to protest but Enderby walked up to Lane who held his ground. 'No one calls me a son of a bitch.'

'I just did!'

'Uh-huh, well, I guess that's because you ain't got any manners. When I cussed, my Ma used to wash my mouth out with soap and water.'

He stepped forward quickly, planting a boot on the startled Magill's instep, pinning his foot to the ground, while he drove the muzzle of the big Dragoon Colt into the man's midriff. Lane made a sick sound, grabbed at his middle, his legs sagging. By then, Enderby had rammed his gun into his belt, grabbed Magill by the shirt collar and dragged the floundering man across to the narrow washbench. A bowl of scummy, cloudy water stood there with a sodden rag hanging over the edge. A piece of worn-down lye soap rested on the bowl's slanting edge.

Enderby grabbed it and the rag while Magill clawed groggily at the bench edge, trying to make his legs strong enough to hold his weight as he gagged for air. Buck rubbed soap into the filthy rag.

He twisted fingers in Lane's curly brown hair, yanked his head back. Magill's mouth was wide open, still sucking air, when Buck shoved the soapy rag in deep and scrubbed briefly, before pushing the man roughly. Magill fell to his knees, gagging and choking, clawing at the rag. When it came free he hawked and retched.

Buck turned to the bug-eyed Renny. 'Get his war bag and things and toss 'em out here. Then saddle his mount for him.'

Renny started to obey, then stopped and looked back belligerently. 'I'm not his slave! Nor yours!'

'You're just helping out, kid, not slaving. Now do it, or maybe you'd like your mouth washed out, too—'

Muttering, Renny Pardoe stomped inside and by the time he came out, Lane was rinsing his mouth at the well, glaring hatred at Buck Enderby. He jumped when his war bag thudded at his feet, gave Renny a menacing stare, then looked back to Enderby. The kid walked over to saddle Magill's horse.

'I won't forget you, Enderby! By God, I won't!'

'Where I come from, we're courteous to all strangers, until we figure 'em out, leastways. Your own fault, Lane. Now get on down to the house. The Senator's waiting.'

Shakily, still spitting occasionally, Magill mounted, lifted the reins, and as he turned his mount's head, spoke to Renny:

'I was tired of nursemaidin' you, anyway. You're always gonna be a pain in the ass, kid, always!' He raked his gaze across Enderby and rode on out.

Buck pushed his hat back on his head. 'Well, kid, just you and me now. Looks like the start of a beautiful friendship.'

Renny snapped his head around. 'You think so? Well, no matter what they told you, I don't want you here, Enderby! But I'm stuck with you for a while, so to start with, *don't call me kid!* I told you that once before!'

Renny turned back into the shack, slamming the door. Buck smiled thinly, went back to his horse, off-saddled and turned the animal into the corral, hanging his rig over the top rail. He shouldered his war bag and carried his sheathed rifle in his other hand as he walked back towards the shack. There was movement at the window, which was a glassless square, covered only by a wooden flap, now propped outwards by a stick.

Renny was waiting for him when he came through the door. The kid held a shotgun he had obviously taken down from a set of wall pegs.

'You better not try to slap me around again!' he hissed.

'I won't, if you don't do anything to deserve a slapping-round.'

'By hell, I mean it, Enderby! You touch me and—'

Buck heaved his war bag into Renny while he was still speaking and the kid staggerered back, struck a chair and floundered wildly, the shotgun waving about. Enderby had the weapon in his own hands in a flash, broke the breech and smiled when he saw it wasn't even loaded.

'Never bluff. kid . . . er . . . *Renny.* You point a gun at someone you better be ready to use it. It don't only have to be loaded, you have to be willing to pull the trigger. Lesson Number One, OK?'

Renny climbed to his feet slowly, ignoring the hand offered by Enderby. He dusted himself off, watching the other warily. 'Don't think I'm scared of you!' he said in a trembling voice.

Buck replaced the shotgun on the wall pegs. 'Don't want you scared of me. Want you to *listen* to me when I speak, do the things I tell you.'

Renny curled a lip. 'You want to boss me around like everyone else, in other words!'

'Well, let's just see how it goes for a couple or three days, huh?'

The kid thinned-out his lips, picked up his hat which had fallen and sat down on the edge of a bunk, Buck guessed it was the one Renny used up here.

'Sun's going down, best get the fire going.' Enderby pointed to the potbelly stove against one wall. 'Don't look to be much wood.'

Renny glared.

Buck shrugged, went outside and returned with an axe. The kid was lounging full length on his bunk now and he stiffened when the other approached, his eyes on the tool. He jumped, yelling, as the axe blade thudded into the frame of the bunk near his head, the whole shebang juddering and shaking. Enderby squatted in front of the stove, began tearing up newspapers.

'By the time I set the kindling, I'll be ready for the first lot of wood,' he said.

Renny stared a moment longer, then Buck looked up and nodded at the axe. 'Almost ready. . . .'

The kid ran a tongue over his lips, kept his gaze on Buck as he swung his legs slowly over the side of the bunk, freed the axe, and then backed out of the door, looking worried.

Buck struck a vesta and applied it to the kindling. As the flames began licking at the paper and twigs, the axe out in the yard began a rhythmic thudding sound.

Enderby smiled. 'Lesson Number Two,' he breathed.

'Listen, I know how to eat my grub without putting most of it in my lap!' complained Renny bitterly at breakfast. 'I can drink my coffee without slurping. I can blow my nose and wipe my own ass . . . I don't need a goddam nursemaid! This is the Old Man's idea, not mine.'

'He's just thinking of your best interests,' Enderby said, forking up some bacon, eggs and beans which he had cooked earlier. The coffee pot was bubbling now and he pointed to it with his fork. 'Get that, will you?'

'No!' Renny made his mouth small and unsmiling, folded his arms across his chest.

Enderby set down his utensils went to the stove, poured himself a cup of coffee, set back the pot to one side of the hotplate and took the coffee back to the table. He blew on it, sipped, and smacked his lips, obviously enjoying it. When he looked up he saw Renny frowning. 'Help yourself to a cup—'

'You coulda brought me one back!'

'Could've, or you could've gotten a cup for both of us. Worked out different, that's all, but sooner you realize you ain't going to be waited on hand and foot the better.'

'Yeah, well, Lane used to bring my grub and coffee into the bunk.'

'Then Lane was a fool and not doing the job he was hired for. You slip him an extra dollar or two?'

The kid flushed and Buck knew he was right.

He finished his meal, drank his coffee and smoked a cigarette. All that time the kid just sat there, sulking, his food growing cold. When he had smoked his cigarette, Enderby collected his own plate and cup, went to the bench outside and washed them up, propping them to dry in the early sun. It was cool and brisk, the day promising to be fine and warm later.

'Come on, let's get started.'

'Too damn cold yet, I'll wait a while.'

'Renny, you can skip breakfast and go hungry for all I care, but we've got work to do, you and me. I'm ready, so you're ready too, like it or not.'

'I don't like it and if you think you can—'

Renny's words trailed off as Enderby stepped into the cabin. The kid was seated on the edge of his bunk now and he looked startled, afraid, as Buck walked towards him. Buck knew the kid was pushing him, trying him out.

He grabbed Renny's hat from a wall peg, jammed

it on his head, hauled him to his feet by his shirt front and started to drag him, flailing and wailing, towards the door.

'My boots! My boots! I ain't got my boots on!'

Enderby shoved him back towards the bunk. 'First thing after your hat you put on when you get up in the morning. Any cowhand knows that, you remember it.'

Struggling into his hand-tooled halfboots, Renny scowled, sniffing a little. 'I don't want to be a goddamn cowboy! I'm not like them! I don't care about ranching!'

'Told your old man?'

'He knows.'

'*Tell* him. He's too busy for a subtle approach.'

Renny paused, spoke sullenly. 'He'll whip me!'

'He might bully you some but if you're not too stupid, you can wait him out and tell him your side. What do you want to be, anyway?'

Renny shrugged. 'Dunno, and I don't care! I don't have to *be* anything! Not with all the money he's got.'

Buck sighed, hauled the kid to his feet and sent him staggering to the door. As the kid straightened. Buck shoved him again and he stumbled over the stoop, fighting for balance in the yard.

'Saddle our mounts, Renny.' He spoke easily, not bullying, but his eyes drilled into the kid and after a meaningless glare, Renny did as he was told.

Enderby asked the kid to show him round and after some bitching, Renny seemed pleased enough to do it. He took Buck to the holding canyons where they put the mavericks or mustangs after they rounded them up, kept them there till they settled down, then drove them down to the ranch for breaking or branding. He showed him a river from a ledge that they had to clamber down to, sweeping an arm around.

'See how far you can see from up here . . . River seems to go on to the end of the world. I . . . I like to look at it from up high.'

Something in the kid's voice made Enderby turn to look at him. He asked quietly, 'Come here often?'

Renny looked sharply at Buck. 'Whenever I can, I'd rather spend the whole day up here than doing ranch chores.'

'Wouldn't get the chores done, though. But, yeah, this is a good place, all right. Reminds me of a pocket of the Smokies, only we got more of a blue hazy look to things back home.'

Renny frowned, was about to speak, but apparently changed his mind.

'Be nice here at sundown,' Buck allowed. 'Looking to the west the way it does.'

'Yeah, it's really something. I've watched the sun set from here a couple times. Wished I had stuff to paint it – or try.' He looked uncomfortable. 'I'm not much good at painting.'

'Is that what you want to do?'

Renny flushed deeper, not looking at him, examining his fingernails. 'I like sketching stuff but, as I said, I'm not much good.'

'Take some lessons, there's colleges you can go to.'

'Huh! Tell that to the old man!'

'You should tell him. I don't suppose he knows

about you liking art?'

Renny shook his head. 'He wants to retire to the ranch near San Antonio after he's through with politics. Wants me to have my own place, this one. And manage the other spreads, like the one in Mexico.'

'Well, he's taking care of your future.'

'Yeah, I know – but I don't *want* to be a damn rancher!'

'Put in a good manager then and go study art.'

Renny jumped up and stood staring out over the river and woods, watching a hawk circling. 'You think it's easy! Just tell him and that's it! But you don't go against Senator Pardoe! He says you do something and you do it! He makes you do what *he* wants.' He added with a vicious twist to his mouth. 'You ought to know that!'

Buck sighed. 'Talk to him, Renny, no one else can do it for you. Keep trying till you get him to listen. You got to walk tall if you aim to get any place at all in this world. My old man taught me that. Maybe I ain't got anywhere much but I can stand up for myself, so I guess that's Lesson Number Three for you to learn. Meantime, I'd better see what else I can teach you.'

'I told you I don't want to know about roping and all that stuff.'

'Uh-huh. How about shooting? You don't have to be a cowboy to know about guns: more you know, the safer they are – you any good with 'em?'

He saw the interest glow in the boy's eyes immediately. Renny shook his head. 'I can shoot a gun. Not too bad with a rifle, but . . . well, I guess I'm pretty hopeless with a six-gun.'

'OK, let's go find a draw somewhere and we'll try you out.'

For the first time, Enderby saw a true smile on the usually surly face.

'You mean it?'

'Renny, I don't much care for just listening to the sound of my own voice. So mostly, I say what I mean.'

Renny grinned widely, cutting loose with a wild whoop as he rowelled with his spurs. 'Follow me!'

The kid was worse than Buck Enderby expected. He fumbled a six-gun, had no idea of balance, held it all wrong so that it jerked and twisted in his fist, once it kicked back so hard it almost hit him in the face.

Using a rifle was a little better but not much. Enderby got him to aim at the dead branch on a tree. Renny hit it twice out of five shots which was OK, but he was rubbing his right shoulder and grimacing in pain now.

'When you shoot, snug that buttplate tight against your shoulder,' Buck told him, demonstrating. 'Snug it in, use your left hand on the fore-end grip – here – and keep pulling back towards your body. Let it loose and you'll throw lead all over the countryside, and have a damn sore shoulder to boot.'

'I've got one already,' Renny said as Buck held out the Winchester towards him, making no move to take it.

Buck grabbed his hands and put the rifle into them, pointed at the broken branch. 'Take it off at the base. Aim each shot, making sure the tip of the blade is dead centre in the V of the rear sight, level with the top of each arm.'

'I told you, my shoulder's sore.'

'There're four killers. Indians, maybe, but don't matter who, coming at you, you gonna tell 'em to wait until your shoulder feels better? *Shoot that branch off the damn tree!*'

Renny gave him a sour, sullen look, lifted the rifle and gingerly placed the butt against his tender right shoulder. Buck stepped behind him, reached around and yanked the gun back firmly. Renny yelled but Buck didn't release the pressure, pushed the kid's head down so his cheek was against the stock.

'Aim and shoot,' he said calmly and when he felt the kid's head moving slightly to line up the sights, he stepped back.

Renny fired and splinters flew from the dead branch. The tree shuddered. The kid lowered the rifle and turned, a broad smile on his face.

'I got it! Right on the base!'

'Three or four more shots ought to do it.'

He didn't seem to notice the sore shoulder now, but Buck had to remind him to use his left hand to help keep the buttplate pressed home firmly. The kid took his time, aiming carefully and cut the branch off the tree with his fourth bullet.

He almost danced with joy.

Buck reloaded the smoking Winchester swiftly.

'Let's see what you can do,' Renny urged.

'Fair enough.' Enderby chose a bunch of pencil-thin twigs at the top of the dead tree. They spread in a fan of about eight.

Buck cut each one in two – in less than five seconds.

Renny merely stared, open-mouthed, then recovered as Buck finished reloading again.

'How are you with a six-gun? I've seen you in action, down in Mexico, but I mean with a fast draw.' He gestured to the Dragoon rammed into Buck's belt. 'That thing must weigh a ton.'

Enderby nodded. 'One I stole after I broke out of jail. It'll knock a bear on his ass but it's way too heavy to carry, anyway, it's cap-and-ball, too slow to reload.'

'Don't you have a Colt single action?'

'Back at Headquarters I guess, never thought about it. They took it before I went to jail. Lend me yours.'

Renny was wearing a shiny Colt .44 six-shooter in a fancy carved holster tied down low on his right hip. He hesitated, then tried to draw it fast and smoothly for Buck's benefit. It was a disaster and the gun fell to the ground. Renny swore and stomped and picked up the gun as if he would hurl it away.

Buck took it off him and rammed it into his belt, butt foremost. The kid glared, tight-lipped, still angry and embarrassed. 'Lousy damn gun! Pa paid seventy bucks for that damn hunk of iron.'

'Renny – that was you, not the gun.' He let that sink in and slowly the kid calmed down. Buck pointed to a rock. 'You want to put a row of stones on top there? About egg-sized or a little smaller.'

'But that's . . . twenty feet away if it's an inch!'

'Longer distance than any gunfight I ever saw, but a good test for accuracy.'

'How . . . how close do you get in a gunfight?'

'Depends, but usually around six to ten feet.'

When the stones were placed, Renny came back and Enderby told him that he found a cross-draw was superior to the dip-and-lift type that the vast majority of men used.

'We didn't run to fancy holsters much in the Smokies. Mostly we just rammed our guns into our belts like this and whipped 'em out fast as we could – like this.'

He drew and turned, twisting so that he was crouching as the gun appeared in his hand, finger depressing the trigger while the edge of his left hand fanned the hammer spur. Stones shattered and rock dust spurted as the draw filled with the whine of ricochets underlying the thunder of the gun. Buck handed the pistol to the wide-eyed Renny to reload.

'You missed two,' the kid gasped.

Enderby nodded. 'Fanning's not accurate, but it's fast, and if you're close to your man you'll usually hit him and the faster the better. Don't you try it, not yet, leastways. We'll shoot steady at arm's length for a spell.'

'I've never seen anyone draw as fast as you.'

There was real admiration in Renny's voice.

And Lane Magill, watching from a ridge through field glasses, would have agreed with him. He had never seen such prowess with a six-gun. He knew that bracing this damn hillbilly was out of the question. If he wanted to nail the sonuver – and he *did*, like you wouldn't believe – it would have to be from an ambush.

Meantime, while he thought about it, he aimed to go draw his time from Pardoe, then go to town and get drunk.

CHAPTER 7

A BETTER MAN?

Buck Enderby couldn't help but compare Renny to himself when he was a sixteen year old.

All his childhood he was skinny, under-fed, wore no shoes and had the seat hanging out of his pants. But he could shoot the eye out of a turkey at fifty yards in bad light and could skin and dress a possum or rabbit for cooking in three minutes flat. He could track a fly across a lava bed, howl like a coyote, cough like a cougar, whistle and chirp like a hundred different species of birds, read the weather and sniff the air and tell whether there was rain a'coming or maybe hail or sleet. He could read most of Nature's signs, cook well enough so that his Pa and brothers hardly ever complained, knew how to build a log cabin and a shelter in the wilderness out of pine boughs or other branches that would protect him in any kind of weather.

If he went hunting and by some ill luck only

wounded his prey – it had happened only twice, the others being all clean kills – he would track down that prey no matter how long it took or what dangers he had to face until he could put it out of its misery. Not because he liked doing it and putting himself in danger but because Pa had taught him it was the right thing to do. '*No critter should be left to suffer unnecessarily. You wound it, you go after it and kill it.*'

Young Bucky – as he was then – didn't want for much. Maybe more grub on the table at times would have been nice and a wolfskin jacket come the bitter Smokie winters, but otherwise he got along quite well. *Self-sufficient, that was how Pa put it. Learn to be self-sufficient, boy, and the world holds no terrors for you. . . .*

Now this kid, Renny Pardoe, not much older than Bucky Enderby when he blew up the still and killed those Revenue men, Renny grew up with plenty of money and plenty of people to take care of him, grant his wishes, or else, if he didn't get what he wanted right away, he soon learned that throwing a tantrum loud enough and long enough would eventually see him win out.

Maybe his father, the Senator, was tired of that now, but the kid had too many long years of being spoiled and being kingpin wherever he was, because of his father and the rich background. He was born into a lucky family and even now, hundreds of miles south of his home state, his luck stayed with him because his father was heading for the Governor's chair and the Pardoes were *Northerners* with all the backing of the Reconstruction to help them on their way.

Buck felt there was some hope for the kid, the Senator himself showed signs that he at least *knew* what was the right thing, even if he didn't practice it much as a politician. Some good was bound to have rubbed off on Renny and it was Buck Enderby's job to bring it to the fore.

Make a better man out of him, was how Senator Pardoe had put it.

Well, it was going to be quite a job. Renny seemed to be trying but he reverted to his old bullying, tantrums and over-bearing manner much of the time. He was keen to learn all about guns and shooting but even there Buck saw some trouble.

Because, face up to it, the kid was only so-so despite his love of firearms. He couldn't seem to get the knack of handling them smoothy, although Pa had always told Buck that it wasn't a thing that just anyone could learn, there must be natural talent there to start with, even just a whisper of it would help.

Well, Renny Pardoe had the desire but not much of the wherewithal to make things happen the way they should.

He was more interested in that aspect of Buck's job than any other, but Buck came down hard on him when he started to poke out his bottom lip, turned surly and sullen, building up to a tantrum.

'Don't try it, kid – yeah, I said *kid* – you act like one, I'm gonna call you one. You want me to call you by your name, then you *earn* that right. You throw a tantrum and I'll make you sorry. Don't like making threats but any I do make, I mean. You should've learned that much.'

Renny glared, was silent a short time, then seemed to brighten, curling a lip. 'I can get you fired any time I want! All I gotta do is tell the Senator you beat me for nothing or some trivial thing, act it up, and you'll be fired. Oh, I can do it, don't you think I can't! I can wear him down to where he'll do what I want just to get a little peace and quiet.'

'Don't doubt it, kid. You've had plenty of practice, I guess.' Enderby started to move towards him and the sneer dropped from Renny's face as he began to back up.

'What . . . what're you doing?'

'Kid, I've told you not to lie, so, you want to tell the Senator I beat up on you, I might as well make sure at least you're telling the truth.'

He reached for Renny and the kid let out a yell, crouching, getting on the far side of the deal table, looking anxious and ready to dodge and make a run for the door. Enderby strode after him steadily with a blank expression but plenty of determination in his movements.

'Wait! Wait! I was only saying what I could do. Not that I was going to do it!'

Buck stopped, hands on hips, looking hard. 'All right. Now, like I said, today we do some cowhand work. If there's time, we'll go out to the draw and try a little more shooting. But the range work first. Savvy?'

Renny tightened his lips but he accepted it with a jerky nod. 'I need to know how to shoot properly,' he said sullenly, capitulating, making one last try.

'I'll show you what I know, then it's up to you. But your old man wants you to learn how to run a ranch so you can take over that side of his business. And he wants you to learn a few ethics – codes, if you like – that'll stand you in good stead throughout your life.'

Renny laughed shortly. 'Man, has he flim-flammed you! He don't give a damn about my future, only his. You ever wonder why he picked someone like you? A hillbilly?'

'Often, but he's paying me, and another thing my Pa taught me was that you always give value for every dollar paid to you. That's something else for you to learn.'

'Why does he think you're such a damn paragon?' He sounded resentful and Enderby shrugged.

'Ask him, I'm not worrying about it any more. Now let's get some grub for a couple of days, saddle-up, and we'll head for the hills.'

'Did your old man put you through this stuff when you were sixteen?'

'Started long before, beatings and all, if I didn't get it right. By the time I was sixteen, kid, I'd killed three men.'

Buck knew immediately it was the wrong thing to say. It sounded like a boast for one thing, but when he saw the change in the kid's face he knew this was the one thing that Renny would latch on to.

This was what Renny Pardoe would base his respect for Buck on.

He suddenly liked the idea of being taught things by a self-confessed killer.

The mustang round-up was violent, dusty and not all that successful. Enderby built a brush-lined trail where he wanted the horses to run, leading down to the camouflaged corral he and Renny had thrown-up, with a crate that opened easily with little pressure, but snapped shut of its own accord with the aid of a long, bent green sapling.

'The broncs charge through and by the time the first is milling around, the last one is in, the gate's closed and we've got 'em,' Enderby explained.

Renny, despite himself, seemed impressed. 'None of the ranch hands have ever used that, far as I know.'

'There's likely a couple know the trick. Just haven't had a chance to put it into practice. Now we go up before sundown to the waterhole, and stay hid in the brush, let the lead stallion check it out and call the others in. Let 'em drink their fill. Water sloshing in their bellies slows 'em just a mite. Then we hit 'em from two sides, yelling and yahooing, waving hats or ponchos, and we push 'em down to this end of the waterhole where they've got no choice but to follow the trail we've made and lined with cut brush. You can use strips of burlap or gunnysacking, but this way's just as good.'

It was simple enough, something Buck had done many times. It went off fine, except the kid got carried away and pulled his Colt and started shooting holes in the sky. The crash of the gun was like slapping a red hot coal under the tails of the mustangs. They took off like they wouldn't stop this side of California. Some in their panic crashed through the brush walls lining the trail. Others laid back their ears and rolled their eyes and charged after the leader way out in front, following the twisting trail.

The corral was less than half full when the stampede was finally over. Sweating, eyes bright, Renny rode across to Buck who was securing the gate frame to the post with strips of rawhide.

'Man! That was something! I don't feel like stopping, can we get another bunch? Seems to be room in the corral.'

Enderby's eyes were like drills. 'There is, because you started shooting. Told you to use your hat or a poncho or the blanket. Gunfire scared the hell outta 'em and they panicked, broke through the brush wall.'

Renny scowled. 'You saying it's my fault we lost some?'

'At least half. Yeah, it was your fault. You want to make some excuse so you don't have to take the blame?'

The kid was ready to blaze back but something in Buck's stern face stopped him and he fought with himself for a few moments, then sighed. 'All right! I just thought it would . . . get them into the corrals quicker.'

'*Listen* to what I say, kid, then do it. Ask your questions afterwards. If I goof, I'll admit it.'

Renny squirmed in the saddle, began to reload his six-gun, keeping his head down so he wouldn't have to look Buck in the face. 'All right, *I* goofed. Make you happy?'

'Why would it make me happy? It means another lesson you haven't learned. We'll leave those broncs, no use trying to break 'em in. You're sure not ready for that.'

Renny snapped his head up. 'We got time for some shooting, then?'

Enderby hesitated, glanced up at the sun, which was well heeled-over towards the top of the mountain. 'OK, we can get in an hour.'

Renny smiled widely, making him look very young, lit up with the excitement of youth.

But they didn't get any shooting in that day, leastways, not in the remote draw.

Riding across the slope after cutting some grass for the captured mustangs and throwing it into the corral, Buck paused, twisted in the saddle, sniffing. 'I smell smoke.'

By the time Renny had made several large sniffing sounds and started to agree, Enderby was riding fast downslope, rowelling his horse. A little startled, Renny followed.

The sun was just tipping the top of the mountain when they arrived at the lineshack, but both of them knew what they were going to find long before then. The shelter for storing winter hay was ablaze, the corral rails had been torn down and the remuda was gone. There was also a small fire burning against the side wall of the linecamp cabin.

'Get that put out!' yelled Buck to Renny as he unsheathed his rifle and spurred his mount around the cabin, he had caught a movement in the timber above.

'Where you going?' Renny called but Buck just yelled at him to put out the cabin fire, and disappeared into the shadowed trees.

He glimpsed the rider weaving through the thinning timber and when the man passed timberline, Buck stood in the stirrups and cut loose with two fast shots from his Winchester. Bark flew from one tree and the other bullet kicked dirt into a brief fountain a couple of feet from the man's horse.

He hipped in the saddle, startled, flung his own rifle up and blazed a couple of shots at his pursuer.

Buck recognized him as Lane Magill, sheathed his rifle and concentrated on catching up with the man. Magill rode for the crest, out in the open now, in the sparse timber and brush. Enderby closed, his horse panting, though more used to mountain work than the fugitive's.

Lane Magill's horse stumbled and although it righted quickly enough, he lost a lot of ground. The man started to panic, emptied his rifle and then dragged out his six-gun, blazing at Buck Enderby. The man from Tennessee dismounted, taking his rifle with him, dropped to one knee and triggered one shot as Magill lashed and rowelled his stumbling mount on to the crest. The horse shuddered, stopped in its tracks, and then toppled sideways and began to slide down the slope. Magill tried frantically to kick free but the horse had slid several yards before he managed it. He rolled, scrabbling for his dropped six-gun on hands and knees.

Buck fired and the bullet kicked gravel into Magill's face. He shouted, reared up, clawing at his eyes. He froze when he clearly heard the clash of the lever on Buck's rifle again. He spun, hands raised shoulder high.

'Don't! Don't shoot!'

He stood awkwardly, gravel scarred, clothes torn. Buck could smell the man from down the slope.

'You look like hell, Magill. What're you trying to do?'

Lane Magill ran a tongue over his lips. 'I . . . I been drinkin' . . . I ran outta dough, started thinkin' how you took my job. Wanted to get you in Dutch with the Senator—'

'So you decided to burn us out, me and the kid.'

Lane showed a little spirit then curled his lip. 'He's a pain in the butt! I couldn't get close to the big ranch, so figured it'd be just as good to run off the remuda here, burn the winter feed supply and the cabin.'

'You're the pain in the butt, Magill. Stay put.'

Enderby started up the slope and Magill turned, glanced at his six-gun lying in the gravel, only a yard or two away. He licked his lips. Buck stumbled on the loose gravel and as he righted himself, Magill started a half-hearted thrust for his Colt, but changed his mind when he saw how fast Buck steadied.

Then, downslope, a rifle crashed three times and dust spurted from Magill's shirtfront. The bullets thrust him back violently. He half twisted, face a mask of agony as his legs gave way and he sprawled, sliding face down towards Enderby.

Buck twisted as he went down to one knee and swore softly. Renny Pardoe was coming up from timberline, a smoking rifle in his hand and a wide grin on his face. Buck looked past him and saw the flames and black smoke below. 'The cabin's still burning!'

Renny glanced casually over his shoulder. 'I emptied a canteen of water on it. Then I heard the shooting and figured you'd need a hand. And you did, didn't you?'

'He wasn't going for his gun! He started to but changed his mind.'

'Yeah? Looked like he was stooping for it to me. Anyway, he's no loss. Never did like the son of a bitch.'

He was standing, panting a little, in front of Buck now, pleased with himself. Until Buck hit him and knocked him down. 'What's that for?' he gasped, rubbing his jaw as he sat up dazedly.

Buck rode past him, racing downslope towards the fire.

CHAPTER 8

RETURN

Kim Preece frowned as she looked at Enderby, now standing by the window and looking out into the ranchyard.

'Well? You can't end it there! What happened? Did you save the line camp?'

Without turning, Buck said quietly, shaking his head, 'Too late, if the kid had done what I told him the cabin might've been OK but—'

'If he'd done what you told him, Lane Magill might still be alive, too.'

He turned to look at her, arms folded. 'Maybe, Renny was right, you know, he was no loss. But, of course, that wasn't the point. He'd shot a man down in cold blood, and was proud of it—'

His voice hardened even as he spoke, remembering his anger at Renny Pardoe that day.

Renny rode back down to the smoking ruins of the line camp, looked around and shrugged.

'Looks like the old man's gonna have to build a new one.'

'That all it means to you?'

'Well, hell, it's no skin off my nose, Buck. Why are you mad at me for shooting Lane Magill? I thought I saved your neck.'

'You didn't.' Buck's voice was curt, like a falling axe blade.

'Well, I did like you told me, snugged that rifle butt well into my shoulder, got that blade sight dead between the V of the rear and—'

'Let it ride, kid, shooting an unarmed man is nothing to be proud of. And if you can't see that, it's not much use me trying to teach you any different.'

'Judas! I'm damned if I understand you!'

'No. We'd better ride down and tell your father what's happened.'

That sobered the kid, wiped the happy look off his face. He was even more unhappy when Buck stayed silent and let him tell the Senator about Magill and the line camp fire.

Pardoe senior swore softly. 'I heard Magill had been cutting-up rough in town, should've had someone kick his butt out of there.' He flicked his gaze to Enderby. 'You're pretty quiet.'

'Renny's job to tell you these things.'

'Hmmmm. Guess you must've taught him something, if he managed to shoot Lane Magill. He was a pretty tough customer.'

Buck said nothing and the Senator frowned. 'Well, you've still got your job to do and another two months left to work off your parole. There're two other line camps you can work out of—'

'No. We'll go back to the one Magill burned out. We can rebuild it, Renny and me.'

'Wait a minute!' snapped Renny, eyes blazing. 'If you think I'm gonna start cutting timber and digging post holes to rebuild that damn camp—'

The Senator flicked his gaze to Buck and then back to the kid. 'If that's what Buck wants to do, you'll do it.'

Renny did plenty of complaining but Senator Pardoe was adamant and he and Buck moved back to the hills the next day, with a buckboard loaded with tools and some spare lumber.

That same afternoon they got to work clearing up the charred timbers and rubbish left from the fire. A small party of cowboys rode by on their way up to the corral in the hills where Buck and Renny had left the trapped mustangs for breaking-in. They grinned and whooped and threw a few taunts at Renny: seeing him actually slaving away at manual work was a new experience for them.

Renny, of course, didn't like it one damn bit.

Not that it mattered. He did what Enderby told him although they had plenty of arguments. But Buck didn't have to slap him around, although with some of the lip he had thrown at him Renny was lucky he was getting round without a large gap in his smile.

After a few days, the kid suddenly started doing things off his own bat. He anticipated tools and materials that were required and went to fetch them instead of having to be coerced or ordered. Buck noticed him taking more care with measurements and lining up planks and frames, even hammering in nails. When he started Renny almost 'choked' the hammer, his hand only a couple of inches from the head. Over and over Buck had told him that the further along the handle he gripped, the more power and control he had over the swings. Instead of wasting handfuls of bent nails, Renny suddenly began punching them straight into the timber with hard, economical strokes. He even sharpened his chisels after supper by firelight.

After the frame of the cabin was up he admitted to Buck that he was 'kind of enjoying this'. Buck reckoned he might break his own arm, but he felt like giving himself a pat on the back . . . *Progress like that was unexpected. But mighty welcome. . . .*

The linecamp when finished looked better than the original and Renny set about making a table. Buck, to keep the mood going, made a set of rustic chairs.

'Good to see something for your efforts, ain't it?' he allowed, one evening when Renny was finishing off the table edge with a hand plane. He planned to carve the legs, too.

'Yeah, yeah! It is.' And the response sounded as genuine as any Buck had ever heard.

Renny still wasn't keen on ranchwork. Making and carving things appealed to his artistic instinct and he had a small collection of charcoal sketches he had done over the time they had been working at the camp. Buck recognized himself cutting the shingles and swinging the door on leather hinges, shaping long nails at the anvil.

'You got talent, Renny. You should talk to the Senator about developing it.'

'Ah, he wouldn't let me do anything about it.'

'Why don't you do a sketch of him? It'll be easy to do from memory, give it to him when we go back to the main ranch. Impress him.'

Renny's face brightened but only briefly, he shook his head. 'Wouldn't work.'

But Buck noticed him sketching something he kept hidden in his spare time.

The kid improved his shooting and handling of guns, even seemed to like the maintenance required to keep them in tiptop condition. He had even gone back to the ranch and brought back a Colt .44 Frontier model pistol for Buck in place of the old Dragoon. He was surprised when Enderby modified the tie down holster, reversed it on the bullet belt and fixed it around his waist so that the butt faced forward.

They had many a friendly discussion about the pros and cons of this as opposed to the regular tie-down holster. Other times, Buck tried to impress on the kid that it wasn't hard to follow a personal code of behaviour.

'All it means is you don't go round prodding every ranny you meet to see if you can beat him to the draw. It's mighty dangerous, specially if he's faster than you. But you need to set yourself some standards, draw the line, if you like, one that you won't let anyone step across.'

'What's your line, Buck?'

Enderby shrugged. 'Nothing I ever think about, it was ingrained in me right from when I was born, I guess. I won't be insulted; won't stand by for anyone trying to cheat me, and if anyone calls me a liar he's already halfway to hell . . . apart from that, I respect women, and men who deserve my respect, and I like to think that most folk respect me, and my code. You've got to work at it, Renny. But it's worth it.'

'How about being . . . fast on the draw?'

'I already told you about that. No one but a fool keeps wanting to try and prove how fast he is with a gun. He'll be dead before long and if he isn't, folk'll learn to hate the sound of his name, and I don't reckon that's any way to live, either, folk cussing your name because the're afraid of you.'

Buck thought that the kid seemed to consider all this and they got along a lot better.

Whether he liked it or not, Buck taught him how to handle ranch chores, showed him animal tracks and what they meant, often according to the type of country where they were found. He showed him stalking and silent hunting and the kid surprised him how easily and skilfully he picked it up.

The thing was, Renny liked the outdoors best, whether it was living under the sky or just for painting and sketching. He had finished his charcoal sketch of the Senator, had gone into a lot of detail, and captured the senior Pardoe's features and expression perfectly.

Then came the day when they rode back to the ranch and Senator Pardoe told Buck Enderby the parole was at an end and he had arranged things that

Buck didn't have to serve out the remainder of his time in the Rangers. It was up to Enderby whether he took advantage of the concession or not.

'If I have a choice I'll ride on out. I've been away too long.'

The Senator looked at him shrewdly. 'Someone waiting?'

Buck nodded briefly and Pardoe looked at him thoughtfully.

'I'm working on a few . . . radical . . . changes to our laws, especially the land laws. Seems I might've trod a little heavily on some toes. There have been a few veiled, well, 'threats' is probably too strong a word but you know what I mean.' Enderby said nothing. 'I could use a bodyguard and personal troubleshooter . . . interested?'

' 'Fraid not, Senator. Sorry.'

Pardoe sighed and didn't pursue it. He paid Buck a thousand dollars for his work with Renny. The Senator seemed pleased, but warily so. He nodded pleasantly enough when he saw the sketch Renny had made of him, looking somewhat surprised.

'*You* did this?' When Renny nodded, Pardoe said, 'Never knew you had it in you, of course, your mother always wanted to paint, she said, but she had other duties that prevented her from doing anything about it.'

'Helping you with your career,' Renny said and it was hard for him to hide his bitterness.

The Senator narrowed his eyes, rolling up the sketch now into a tight cylinder. 'Something like that,' he said curtly, tossed the sketch casually on to a chair and then proffered a hand to Buck Enderby. 'If ever you're back this way, Buck.'

Renny walked down to the corrals and watched Buck saddle up. '*Will* you be coming back this way?'

'Sometime maybe. Got a woman waiting for me in Tularosa Valley, Renny, it'll all depend.'

'Well . . . I'd like to think I've got a woman waiting for me, too, but—' There was a dreamy look in the kid's eyes that puzzled Buck. 'Anyway, wish you luck.' They shook hands and Buck swung into the saddle. As he turned to ride out of the big ranch yard, he said, 'Maybe we could have a shootout one day, you and me, friendly, I mean. At targets. Just to see who's fastest—'

Buck Enderby looked down at him soberly. 'I don't think so, kid.'

And Renny knew he had said the wrong thing: now he had to try and figure out *why* it was the wrong thing.

'And that's still not the end of it,' Kim Preece said after a long pause, going to stand at the window beside Enderby. She slipped a hand through his arm, waited for him to turn and looked up into his face. 'You came home broke and with that bullet wound—'

He half-smiled. 'Got as far as a place called Segundo, counted up my money and decided that a thousand bucks wasn't enough for my stake in this place.'

'You'd be *working*! I keep saying, you don't need money!'

'I say I do. Anyway, there was this new saloon in Segundo. Had a big section set aside, just for gambling—' He felt her grip tighten on his arm. 'Roulette, keno, faro, poker, any dice game you liked—'

'Don't tell me!'

He nodded grimly. 'Yeah. Figured I could beat the house, build that thousand into something worthwhile. Didn't take me long to realize the game was fixed and I called out the houseman—' He spread his hands and indicated his bandaged side. 'Turned out the sheriff owned a share in the saloon so I had to light out fast before I could see a sawbones.'

Kim sighed, shaking her head. 'You and your stupid damn pride!'

It was three weeks before Buck Enderby was riding again and able to draw and shoot the pip out of an ace-of-spades in the blink of an eye. He ruined a whole deck of cards, sticking each one into a crack on top of a corral post. Kim was really impressed when he shot two in half – edge-on.

'That's just showing-off,' he said, reloading deftly. 'See how long it took me to line up the sights and steady my hand? I'd've been dead long before I could pull the trigger.'

'It must have impressed Renny.'

He lifted his gaze slowly. 'Never showed him, I didn't think I'd made that good a man out of him. Didn't want him to fix on to the fast draw at all. Just wanted to teach him competence with firearms and how to handle them safely. He took to guns like a duck takes to water.'

'You sound . . . worried.'

He shrugged. 'Depends if his father can hold him in check.'

'You . . . think he might . . . use what you've taught him, the wrong way?'

Buck smiled crookedly. 'Be more than surprised if he doesn't try.'

'Then why? Why did you teach him at all!'

'Because if he went on swaggering around the way he was, knowing nothing, but *thinking* he knew it all, he'd be dead in a week.'

She smiled and squeezed his arm. But her smile faded when he prised her fingers loose and turned so she could grasp his left side. 'Never hold my gun arm, Kim.'

Surprised, she swept an arm around the ranchyard with two cowhands working down by the barn, cattle grazing in the pastures, the wrangler leading some of the remuda down to the river to drink. A peaceful Western scene.

'Out here?'

'*Any*where, Kim, just never cramp my gun arm.'

As he walked away towards the tool shed she frowned: she didn't really know this man she was going to marry at all, she thought.

And it scared her.

It was in the middle of Fall when Buck Enderby rode in from the range one day and saw the strange horses hitched to the corral rails.

He had been thinking of the coming wedding, now set for 15 November, and he had to wrench his mind back to the present. The weeks had passed pleasantly.

He was enjoying the ranch work and had slowly been worn down by Kim so that he agreed to name a wedding day. He still felt he should be contributing cash towards this, all his life he had worked for what he had and had never accepted anything he didn't feel he had earned one way or another.

Kim Preece had inherited this ranch from her father and she had lost a brother in the War, he felt awkward about just walking in and being given fifty percent of it simply because he was marrying her.

But as he dismounted and saw the two men in the shade on the porch all thought about weddings and ranch shares fled his mind.

One man was Bud Brosnan, the other Cord Brewster.

He walked across slowly, carrying his rifle. Bud Brosnan lifted a hand but Brewster merely sat there nursing a cup of coffee, cigarette slanting from his lips. Badges glinted on both men's shirts.

'Long time no see, Buck,' Brewster said as Enderby reached the porch steps. He lifted his cup. 'Your woman makes fine coffee.'

'How'd you find me, Cord?'

'Little bit of askin' around, little bit of deduction, lot of hard ridin'.' Brewster smiled thinly.

Enderby didn't take his eyes off him. 'Which leaves me to ask "why".'

'Yeah, little trouble, Buck, the senator's been shot.'

'Hell, is he dead?'

Brewster shook his head. 'No, in a coma, though, and the kid's missin'.'

CHAPTER 9

RIDE TO THE RIO

Buck Enderby knew what a chance he was taking going back to Mexico, they had long memories down there and although the politicians might have done some sort of a deal and agreed to allow his parole, it didn't mean the men of the Border Patrol felt the same way.

He held back in rough country until dark, rode the few miles down to the river, but again halted amongst some rocks. Badly wanting a smoke, he put the urge from him, sat and waited with mosquitoes and his horse stamping irritably every so often as the bugs bit hard. Straining to see, for there was only starlight, no moon yet, he watched the sluggish water and its vague reflections.

Two hours passed and there was no sign of a patrol. He knew this area from a time when he and some others rustled a bunch of horses after hearing the Mexicans were paying up to forty US dollars per head, right after the war ended. It proved to be a myth, they got only fifteen dollars a horse, but they made a little extra by waylaying a pay-train bound for an army post and found two places to cross the Rio in virtual safety from detection by the patrols. This was one of them.

The night was full of sounds, but only those he would expect to hear. So, rifle in hand, hammer cocked and a cartridge in the breech, he rode out of the boulders. The river was chest-deep on the horse here, except for a short distance in the middle when the animal had to swim hard.

Buck was looking around constantly, becoming slightly dizzy, in fact, from so much head movement, but they made it safely across. He wasted no time. Even as the horse heaved up out of the Rio on to the bank with a panting grunt, he touched the spurs to its flanks, tugged the reins left and rode into a draw whose entrance was invisible from the river.

He dismounted, trouser legs wet, the horse shaking droplets over him in some kind of protest. He automatically reached for tobacco and papers, squatted down and rolled a smoke, wondering if he had been stupid to make this ride down here.

Brewster hadn't gone into a lot of detail about the Senator's shooting. But there was enough to make it pretty clear that Renny had done it.

'Seems the Senator riled him somehow,' Brewster said. 'There were strips of paper scattered all over the room and when we put 'em together, it turned out to be some kind of sketch of the Senator. Torn up by someone feelin' mighty mad, I reckon.'

'The kid drew it in charcoal,' Buck told him. Kim had joined the group and Chip Riley and a Ranger known as 'Trapper' came up from the barn with another man named Conner. Buck was surrounded by Rangers. 'Kid wants to learn to be an artist, I told him he'd have to ask the Senator himself about it. Maybe he did and Pardoe said "no".'

'Why would the Senator want to refuse him to develop a talent he already has?' asked Kim.

'Senator has other plans, aims to be Governor. Wants the kid to manage the cattle business for him so he can get on with his political career.'

'That's selfish!'

Buck shrugged and Brewster said, 'Well, looks like Pardoe might've got the kid well and truly riled-up by tearing up the sketch. Kid must've gone plumb loco and shot him, then lit a shuck.'

He looked expectantly at Enderby who frowned and seemed dubious.

'He's a spoilt brat, ain't he?' put in Brosnan. 'It's the way a kid like him would react if he didn't get his own way.'

Buck saw Kim watching him closely and he shook his head slightly. 'I dunno. He's got a pretty short fuse but I thought he was learning a bit of control.'

'Maybe with you,' Brewster said. 'He likely knew if he didn't go along with what you were s'posed to be teachin' him you'd slap him down.'

'I didn't slap him around for the hell of it. Fact, I hardly laid a hand on him. He knew how far he could push me, but I felt he was learning.'

'Likely panicked,' Brewster said and Buck had to agree it could happen.

Renny was volatile and he would have had to work himself up to find the courage to ask the Senator about sending him back East for a college course in art. He could well have been at breaking point, just with tension, and thrown a tantrum. Only this time he had thrown a gun, too.

And Buck had taught him how.

'Is there anything to say it *was* Renny who shot the Senator?'

'Well, seems the blacksmith was shoeing a horse at his forge, which is a fair way from the house, the other hands were on round-up on the range. He thought he heard a shot but couldn't be sure, what with his hammering and the forge roaring. Then next he saw the kid storming out of the house with his war bag and rifle, headed for the corrals. He watched him ride out, called to ask where he was going but the kid didn't answer.'

'Did he say how Renny looked?'

Brewster hesitated briefly, nodded. 'Wild, he said. Riled and wild, near gutted his horse spurrin' away—'

Enderby's mouth tightened. 'Damn! Sounds like Renny's reaction . . . leastways, how he *used* to react.'

'You weren't there to keep him under control, Buck,' Kim said quietly and he nodded. 'You can't possibly blame yourself for this!'

She knew she was wasting her time, it's exactly what he was doing. *And he would go looking for Renny Pardoe! Even though the wedding was only three weeks away.*

'I thought I'd taught him better,' Buck said, only half-aloud, flicking his gaze towards Brewster. 'Why'd you come here, Cord?'

'Two reasons: figured you'd like to know for one, thought it just possible the kid might run to you, for two.'

'He didn't know where to find me.'

'Mentioned you said you had a woman waiting in the Tularosa,' Brewster pointed out. 'It's what gave us a starting point when I decided to come check.'

'Well, I did say that, I guess, but he hasn't been here. And I don't think he'd come anyway. He'd be smart enough to know you might look up this way.'

Bud Brosnan stood impatiently. 'Well, where's he gonna go? You're the nearest thing to a friend he has—'

Enderby said nothing and Kim, giving him a sober look, said, straightfaced, 'I'll go make the supper.'

When she had gone inside, Enderby sat down on the porch steps and rolled a cigarette. Brewster came and sat beside him.

'You got an idea where he's gone, ain't you?'

'Not much, he could be anywhere. You say this happened a week ago?'

'Eight days, and no one's seen the kid.' When Buck didn't make any comment, Brewster went on, 'There was a third reason I came to see you, you know the Senator kinda fixed things so you didn't have to serve out those last four months in the Rangers. . . ? Well, it was given the *unofficial* OK, but Pardoe has a lot of enemies and those who want to disband the Rangers saw it as favouritism and they've reneged now he's out of action.'

Buck snapped his head around. 'What—?'

Brewster smiled thinly. 'Sorry, Buck, old pard, but you gotta work out that four months service or it's back to the San Antonio stockade.'

Enderby's eyes were hard and pinched down. 'You're enforcing it, Cord?'

Brewster lifted both hands in a helpless spread. 'Hey, I just do what I'm told. I'm a Captain of Troop, but like I told you, it don't mean much. There's plenty over me, I thought you'd want to help anyway, Buck.'

'Maybe . . . I had hoped I was rid of that kid.'

Brewster laughed. 'The hell you were! You'd've been checkin' on him, see what kinda job you'd done with him. Well, now looks like he needs your help again. Only this time it's more serious.'

Buck stood and walked into the house without saying anything. Brosnan frowned at Brewster.

'Think he'll help?'

Brewster nodded, looking grim. 'He'd better!'

Brewster and his three men found room in the bunkhouse for the night. When they had left the house after supper, Kim, who had been very quiet during the meal, watched Enderby smoking over his coffee and said quietly.

'You're going to look for Renny, aren't you?'

'Have to. I guess you can say I made him what he is, so I'm responsible for his actions.'

'How stupid can you be, Buck!' She almost stamped her foot she was so angry. '*You* didn't make him anything! What he is now is because of whatever happened to him between the time he was born and the moment he . . . shot his father. If he did—' He snapped his head up at that but said nothing. 'You aren't to blame! *You don't need to go!*'

He sighed, told her about the rescinding of the decision that he didn't have to serve out his time in the Rangers.

'You believe that?' she snapped.

'Yeah, why wouldn't I?'

'Brewster's using you! Anyone can see he's that kind of a man! He's in a bind, can't find Renny. He thinks you either know where the kid would go or you can make a much better informed guess than he can!'

'Well, don't matter which, Kim, I'm going to look for Renny.'

She was pale, her face tight. 'You think you know where he might be?' He nodded but, although she waited, he did not tell her his thoughts. 'Buck, our wedding is in three weeks. *Three weeks!* For God's sake, doesn't that mean anything to you?'

'Of course it does, Kim, I might be able to get back by the fifteenth, with a little luck. I'll sure try.'

She stood, small fists clenched down at her sides. 'Buck, if you go now, don't bother coming back! I mean it. This is the last straw! For years I've put up with your restlessness and your uncertainty about whether you want to get married or not. Now . . . now when everything is arranged, you're riding out again *and you damn well don't need to!*'

'You know I do, Kim.' He stood and started

towards her but she shook her head, eyes glistening, backing away, a hand stretched out in front as if she would push him back. 'Kim, please try to understand—'

'I do understand, Buck, I finally do understand! You don't really want to get married at all. You just want a place you can come back to after you've finished your wanderings. Well, from now on, it's out of bounds to you! *Do you understand that?* There's no ready-made home for you here anymore! Pack your things and take them with you. You'll have no reason to come back here then—'

'I will, you'll be here.'

She paused with the door partly open, tears coursing down her face now. 'No. I won't be here, Buck, not for you! There'll be *nothing* here for you!'

The door closing sounded like a dull gunshot.

And here he was in Mexico, following a hunch that he wasn't even sure would produce results.

But he *had* to be here. Had to find the kid before he went overboard and got himself killed.

There had been a kind of trail leading him here.

Riding south from Tularosa, making for the part of the Rio he hoped to cross without being discovered, he had pulled into a town called Chaco Flats, just over the line in Texas. He needed supplies and wanted to get some portable oats for the horse for later.

In the saloon bar, while having a couple of beers before hitting the trail again, there was a lot of talk about a gunfight that had taken place a week earlier.

Seemed this kid had ridden in, and Buck had no doubt it was Renny from the description, had let it be known that he would pay for information or even a guide to help him cross into Mexico without the authorities knowing.

It was a dangerous thing to do openly, letting folk know you had money to throw around and, of course, some of the hard boys set the kid up. One man called Boone said he was in with a smuggling gang who could get Renny across for a couple of hundred dollars. The kid had agreed and foolishly made a rendezvous with Boone on the outskirts of town after dark.

Boone had two companions, a breed calling himself 'Romano' and another blocky whiteman named Gannon. They surrounded the kid when he dismounted and demanded all his money.

The kid told them he had it in a bank and could draw it only by Bank Draft when needed. He only had a hundred dollars on him – the down-payment for his passage to the Rio. He would pay the other hundred just before they crossed into Mexico. At least that was the deal, he thought.

Boone was the one who called him a liar and made the mistake of lunging for him. So Boone was the first to die.

Renny's gun blazed and punched Boone back a yard-and-a-half as two bullets slammed into the smuggler. He dropped to one knee and Romano's lead passed over his head. Renny fanned the gun hammer, slapping off all four remaining shots. Romano caught one in the belly and one in the hip and lay there screaming as Gannon turned and made a run for it but was smashed off his feet by Renny's last bullets.

The gunfire brought people running but by that time the kid had faded into the night. Romano lived long enough to tell what had happened, asking for a priest so he could confess all of his sins. He died before the priest reached him.

In El Paso, Buck had picked up a trace of Renny again.

The kid had taken on a few beers and someone had slipped him something in the last glass. He had realized what had happened when nausea and dizziness sent him reeling. He thrust his fingers down his throat and made himself vomit. It didn't rid his body of all the drug, but it left him enough good sense to climb on his horse and make a run for it. Two saloon men came after him. He rode one down, breaking the man's leg and four ribs, shot the other from the saddle, smashing his collar bone.

After that, the kid disappeared.

So Buck followed his original hunch that Renny was making for Mexico to see Rina Diego, the girl he had had all the trouble with months earlier when Enderby had first rescued him.

Renny had said once he wished he had a girl waiting for him somewhere and in one of the lonely night camps up in the woods when he had been learning wilderness survival from Buck, he had confessed that he loved Rina Diego.

'OK, so I deflowered her. It just happened, Buck. I never had that intention, but I didn't think it was right she had to marry some old geezer nearly sixty years old just because her father said so. She said she loved me, and well, it happened and then everything blew up. We never got a chance to see each other again. But maybe some day I'll go back for her.'

'Be riding into no end of trouble, Renny,' Enderby had told him.

The kid had nodded, looked pensive, then tapped his gun butt. 'At least I could defend myself now.'

It had never been mentioned again but Buck had a notion Renny Pardoe just might go back and try to claim Rina for himself. The *hidalgo*, of course, had rejected her as damaged goods, insulted, and by tradition Rina's father would have had to make some kind of recompense. He would see his daughter as a liability now, of no use in the Spanish way of arranging marriages so that a union would be beneficial to all parties.

But he would still guard her zealously and would likely set his *caballeros* on to Renny if he went after the girl. The kid must feel mighty cocky now after those two shootouts on the way down, but if he wasn't where Enderby had found him the last time, Buck knew *he* would have to approach Don Diego and the bullets would fly.

But he would get Renny back to the States safely. Somehow.

He *had* to.

CHAPTER 10

GRINGO'S GUNS

He was forced to keep to the lonely trails, and any trail in that part of Mexico was not only lonely but downright dangerous.

It was loosely called *bandido* country but there were more dangers than just the bandits who made a brutal and blood-thirsty living there. The loners and outcasts, rejected even by the bandit gangs; army deserters; it was said in one section of the foothills of the Cordillera that there were men who ate other men. There were jaguars and mountain lions and an occasional black bear which was often sought by American hunters for its unusual hide as a trophy.

So the wingless vultures who prowled this dangerous area often had a windfall when a lone, poaching *americano* came hunting with his big expensive guns.

Buck Enderby was aware of all this. But he had chosen to ride through this land because it would save him many miles of following the normal, safer trail which clung tenuously to the long mountain range, ignoring the high and low passes. He rode with his rifle butt on his knee, a bullet in the chamber, finger on the trigger guard. His head moved constantly and his belly tightened at every movement he saw: a highly coloured bird flitting from branch to branch in a tree-top swaying in the wind; the rustle of some snake or lizard in a patch of chaparral or mesquite; a flash of grey hide as a furred animal slunk away into the deeper shadows.

He had taken the precaution of bringing two big saddle canteens and had filled both before venturing into this country of high danger and high thirst. A man without water here was a dead man. Despite his alertness, when he stopped to drink, without dismounting, his rifle across his thighs, he missed the one movement that almost cost him his life.

It was high up the slope, on a sheer rock wall overlooking the entrance to a narrow pass: a flash of sunlight searing along a rifle barrel.

Once through the pass there would still be plenty of risk, but he would have left the worst area behind. Having slaked his thirst, he corked the canteen and was hanging it over his saddlehorn when the metal bottle was torn from his grasp, exploding water all over him. Hair-trigger instincts working, he plunged the other way out of the saddle. But the horse shied, startled by the cracking echoes of the rifle shot. It threw him wildly and his Winchester hit a rock, jarred from his grip.

He landed in bushes which broke his fall but branches tore at his clothes and he shielded his face.

He struck a thick branch and rolled awkwardly. The bushwhacker's rifle blasted again in several shots, between him and his own Winchester which was lying in loose gravel several yards down the slope, sliding with the eruptions of dirt caused by the bullets landing near it.

Enderby threw himself backwards, palming up his six gun, noting that his horse had had the sense to plunge into the brush for cover. He frowned, looking up at the drifting gunsmoke high up on the pass wall. That *hombre* up there was using up a lot of lead. Wisely enough, perhaps, but the men who frequented this country seldom had bullets to spare and didn't waste them. That's why so many men were found shot in the back around here. And that rifle sounded in good condition. Not a gun that might have belonged to a straying hunter who had fallen foul of the local killers, he thought. It didn't have that hard snap that the big game cartridges had . . . No, it sounded like a Winchester in good condition, definitely not a Henry with its poor-velocity rimfire ammunition.

He figured that man up there wasn't just one of the outcasts, short on brains and long on murderous intent. This might be worth looking into, not that he had much choice. He was out of six gun range here. He would have to get closer if he wanted a shot at his man.

Even while he was silently voicing these thoughts, his brain was a step ahead of him and, on his belly, he worked his way under the brush to where his horse waited. He was tempted to leap into the saddle and make a wild run for heavier timber, but instead, reached up and flipped his coiled lasso off the saddlehorn.

Then he picked up a heavy fallen branch and tossed it into the brush a little below and off to his right. It drew fire and while the man was blasting the chaparral, Buck thrust his left arm through the coils of the rope and slung it over his shoulder. Crouched double, he ran to his left, leaping a log and almost falling, but he righted himself and pounded on.

Heart racing, he didn't slow down, he went up the slope fast, working under a slight overhang that he hoped would shield him from the man above. The rifle fired a short volley and then was silent and Buck knew the man was looking for him and would be alert for any movements on the periphery of his vision. He bellied down and crawled under the brush, working his way around until he was away from the trail that led into the pass. By now the bushwhacker would be mighty nervous, not knowing where he had gone.

Once he was sure he was in back of the slope where the man was, Buck started climbing in earnest. Sweat darkened his shirt, ran down his neck and face as he clambered over time-riven rocks, slipped in loose scree, going to ground and freezing until the miniature landslides had stopped. They raised a little dust but it would be hard to see through the cloud of powdersmoke that hung around the wall where the killer lurked. He would be watching the rear slope now but would have to divide his attention between that and the area where he had last seen his quarry.

Buck rested, heart hammering, looking out through a gap in the sparse timber over the sun-beaten land. Then he jumped a foot in the air, or it felt like he did, when a rifle blasted only a few feet away, above and off to his right.

He had come higher than he thought! There was a ledge here, jutting out from the wall. It had been unseen from below because it was the same colour rock as the wall and its contours had faded into the bigger area.

Buck slid across carefully, set down the rope so it wouldn't drag against twigs and warn the man. There, only four feet below, stretched out on the rock on a blanket with an open carton of cartridges beside him, surrounded by empty brass cases, was the bushwhacker. He wore *vaquero* clothes and a large hat.

Buck dropped down to the ledge and the man started to spin around but the Colt butt smashed in the felt of the big *sombrero* and cracked against the man's skull. He slumped unconscious. Buck knelt on one knee, Colt reversed in his grip now, and turned him on to his back. He was staring down into an unfamiliar but well-fed Mexican face when he heard the gun hammer behind him click as it drew back to full cock.

'*Señor*, you should know that the *vaqueros* of Don Diego never travel alone! *Adios, gringo*!'

Buck's legs snapped like springs, hurling him back and across the body of the man he had knocked out. And even as his Colt swept around and blasted a fraction of a second before the Mexican's rifle, he thought: *Hell, there were two of them! No wonder there were so many bullets spraying the countryside!*

By then, the man on the rim above had been jarred upright by Buck's bullet and he stepped forward with shaky steps, his tooled leather boot sliding off the edge. He twisted as he fell, struck the narrow part of the ledge and his body bounced off and over to drop silently three hundred feet into the pass below.

Buck got to his feet, every nerve-end screaming, he had nearly died that time! *Don Diego's vaqueros,* the dead man had said.

The Mexican beside him groaned a little and Buck saw there was blood crawling down out of his hairline. He figured that *hombre* would have one hell of a headache when he came round.

When the man opened his eyes, there were dark veils still to be torn aside before full consciousness would return. His head pounded. His eyeballs felt as if they were being forced out of their sockets. He couldn't move his hands . . . or his feet! He jerked his eyes open properly and focused on what lay before him.

Then he screamed.

Several times his scream of pure terror echoed and re-echoed through the pass and over the high crests of the Cordilleras.

He was suspended upside down by the ankles from a branch on a tree whose roots – to him, anyway – didn't seem to have a very good hold on the parched soil beside the ledge where he had lain in ambush for the *gringo.* Something prodded him hard in the ribs, making him gag as he dragged down breath for yet another scream. Saliva dribbled upwards from his mouth and into his nostrils. He shook his head violently as he sneezed and saw Buck Enderby sitting casually on the edge of the flat rock nursing a rifle, the Mexican's own rifle, which he had just used to poke him in the ribs hard enough to tear flesh.

'*Amigo*, you are between a rock and a hard place, and if you want to see *how* hard, just take a look at that red smear down there and see if you recognise your *compadre*.'

The Mexican felt his gorge rise as he saw the broken corpse far below. His body began to twist against the lay of the rope, It made him even more dizzy.

'*Señor*! Please! I only do what I am told!'

'Sure, I savvy that . . . Don Diego, right?'

Surprised, the Mexican swallowed and nodded.

'He told you to lay for *me*?' Enderby was puzzled as to how the ranchero could have known he would be coming.

'He say *someone* will come after the *chuquillo*. But, *aiyee*! He is not the child anymore! He fight like a man, very *macho hombre*, with his gun—'

Sweat was blinding him and he didn't really mind its sting, at least he couldn't clearly see that terrible drop beneath him. Maybe this gringo would let him go if he told him what he wanted to know.

'Did they kill him?' Enderby asked grimly.

'No, *señor*, we are so shocked how this *muchacho* fight, that he get away. And he take the *Señorita* Rina.'

Buck didn't know whether to feel pleased or not

that he had guessed right. The damn kid, way over-confident, had done what he expected! He had come looking for 'his girl' and he had taken her by force from a bunch of hardcase Mexes.

'You know where he went?'

The man was silent and Buck poked him hard in the ribs again, used the rifle to prod his shoulder and set him spinning and swaying violently. The man screamed but his words were incoherent. Buck waited patiently for the swinging to lose momentum and finally reached out and stopped the man. He had vomited and was half choking and spitting.

'Didn't hear you, *amigo,* ' Enderby said lifting the rifle.

'No! No! Please! I don't know where he go, *I swear*!' The Mexican croaked. 'I could very much appreciate a drink of water, *señor, por favor*?'

'Let's finish our talk first. Now where did Don Diego send his men?'

The man was in two minds now, he was obviously afraid of Don Diego, but he was terrified of this *gringo* so calmly sitting on the edge of eternity, throwing questions at him.

It didn't take long for terror, and thirst, to win over fear and in the end, Buck had trouble shutting the man up.

Now he was a long way south of the place where he had been ambushed.

He knew where he was going, but still couldn't be certain how reliable the information was the Mexican bushwhacker had given him. The man, he said his name was 'Chico', had almost died of a heart attack and was a true mess by the time Enderby pulled him back to the safety of the ledge and untied his hands. He left Chico's ankles tied, something to keep him busy after Buck rode out.

Chico had told him how the raging Don Diego had despatched a group of his best gunfighters and trackers to find the fugitives. Rina had left a note for her father, telling him that she *wanted* to go with Renny Pardoe, to the *Estados Unidos* where they would be married. With an added edge to the shame she already felt, she confessed that she was pregnant by Renny and hoped that one day she would be able to bring Don Diego's grandchild to the *rancho.*

Don Diego's reaction was a mixed one of rage and sadness. He burned with the shame Rina had brought to his name and family and swore she would *never bear the bastard child of this worthless gringo.*

'*Kill them both!*' had been his original order but by the time the caballeros were ready to ride on the trail of the fugitives he had changed his mind. '*Kill only the gringo. Hold the girl somewhere, and I will tend to her personally!*'

The strange thing, according to Chico, was that Renny's trail led in the direction of the high village of Gallatera where Enderby had rescued Renny months earlier from Mexican kidnappers.

It was late afternoon when Buck approached Gallatera again and he could hear the guitar music and drunken singing from the cantinas as he rode down the twisting trail across the face of the mountain. *Why would Renny come back here?* It wasn't likely he had made any friends from that other time. No, 'friends' in Gallatera were more likely to hold him hostage, especially the girl, and see how much they could squeeze out of Don Diego and Senator Pardoe. Taking *gringos* hostage was a lucrative business in these hills.

Something had drawn him back here, and it was possible that Buck was arriving too late to be of help. Don Diego's crew might have already caught up with Renny.

But he had to check, even if it meant placing himself in danger.

He hitched his horse outside a darkened *tortilla* shop and entered the din and smoke and smells of the cantina next door. By the time he reached the bar, the guitars had stopped playing in mid-note as a swarthy hand slapped the strings tight, smothering them, and the singing ceased as all eyes turned to the lone *gringo.* Then a faint murmur started up and Buck knew he had been recognized. He lifted a hand.

'No trouble, *amigos,* just a little information and if I get it, perhaps I will buy drinks all round.'

That promise didn't seem to have any effect, they merely stared in blank silence. Figuring he had nothing to lose, and putting his back to a chipped adobe wall, he asked his questions, and right away saw that Don Diego's name carried more than just weight up here.

Fear was a tangible thing in the smoky room.

'Come on. Have Don Diego's men arrived yet?' Still no answer. 'How about the young *gringo* and

Don Diego's daughter?'

There were sharp suckings-in of breath at that and the crowd turned its back on him. And he knew there was too much fear here for his small promise of a free drink to have any effect. He wasn't loco enough to offer a cash reward of any stature, for he would never walk out of here alive. As it was, he sensed hostility and he decided discretion was the best move, and started around the wall for the batwings.

No one stopped him and he walked with a hand on his Colt to where he had hitched his weary horse. The gun whispered out of leather as a shadow moved in the alley between the tortilla shop and the cantina.

'Please, *señor*!' a man said hoarsely. 'I can tell you about the young *gringo*, but you give me the pesos you would have spent buying tequila for those drunks in the cantina, eh?'

Enderby relaxed slightly. A sneak's greed, well, it wouldn't cost him much, but he didn't lower the gun. He used his other hand to reach into his pocket for a silver five-*pesos* coin. He held it up and a little light glinted from the metal.

'Talk away, *amigo*.'

'You . . . you pay no matter what I tell you?' The man was mighty nervous and Buck agreed he would pay. He saw the man look around furtively. 'The old adobe where you come before . . . they went there.'

'Still there?'

The man hesitated. 'I think . . . the *gringo* only . . . they kill him.'

CHAPTER 11

DOS GRINGOS

The old adobe ruins were in total darkness when Enderby made his way slowly down the slope to the hollow behind them. His Colt was in his holster but he carried the Winchester, loaded, thumb ready to cock the hammer.

Faintly, below and around the other side of the rise now, he could hear guitar music and off-key singing again in the Gallatera cantina. He had made sure no one had followed him up here but he checked again before reaching the rear door which had been battered down since last he was here. The roof hadn't been fixed very well and allowed starlight to wash faintly over the earthen floor.

He made out the dark, shapeless bulk of someone huddled on his side, facing the wall.

Buck mouthed a curse. *Damn! Too late to save the kid.*

He stepped forward and his boot encountered a

dry twig from the roofing materials. It cracked dully. He froze.

Instantly, the shape against the wall spun in his direction and a six gun blasted, the powder flash lighting the room for an instant. Even as he flung himself outside and the bullet tore a spray of adobe from the damaged frame, he glimpsed Renny Pardoe.

The kid had blood streaking his face. Dark rivulets had crawled down from under the red-spotted bandanna he had tied around his head. The echoes of the shot were slamming at Buck's ears as he called:

'Renny! It's Buck! Hold your damn fire!'

He heard the gun hammer cock and flattened against the wall again but no shot came. Instead, he heard Renny's hoarse voice: 'You took your damn time getting here!'

'You had a good lead. Lucky for me you did your business at Diego's *rancho* first, then headed this way. I was already halfway here by then. . . .' Enderby knelt beside the kid and eased him around. 'How bad're you hit?'

'Whacked me in the head, feels like a mule kicked me. Can't see all that well.'

'Better than being dead, like they told me you were.'

'Yeah, it knocked me out and there seems to have been a great deal of bleeding. They rode out and left me.'

'Taking Rina with them. . . .'

Renny's breath sighed out and Buck helped him to his feet. His boots dragged as he took him out the door to the hollow where he had left his horse. He gave the kid water, propping him with his back against a rock.

'Why the hell did you come back here?'

Renny was silent a short while, then he shrugged. 'Had to shoot my way outta Don Diego's. You'd've been proud of me. Remembered all you told me.'

'You fanned your gun back in Chaco Flats and I told you it was too dangerous to do that when you don't have much experience.'

'Aaah . . . it worked.' He looked sharply at Enderby. 'You really been working at trailing me, huh?'

'Renny, you shot your father who happens to be a State Senator and . . . what's wrong?'

'The Senator's been shot?' Buck hadn't yet heard the kid call Pardoe 'Dad' or 'Pa'.

'You shot him according to Brewster. . . .'

'Who's Brewster?'

'Don't give me that, kid! You know him, Captain of Rangers.'

Renny shook his head. 'Only know Cap'n Nathan Cord.'

'That's him. Brewster's his real name. Now the Sen . . .'

'The Senator had him fired, with some of his men,' Renny cut in. 'He found out they were taking graft and working a few other deals with bounties s'posed to be paid over and they put 'em in their own pockets, he's under pressure. Lot of his rivals want to close down the Rangers and revert to the old State Police. The Senator did some investigation and fired

Cord, or Brewster, whatever his name is, and a lot of others so his political enemies wouldn't have reason to expose them and so get the Governor's OK to disband the Texas Rangers entirely. He wanted to get rid of the bad eggs first.'

Buck was very still now. 'When was this?'

'Before I left, the Senator had just received confirmation that the men had been fired.'

'And he was OK? There was no argument and you didn't shoot him?'

'Hell, no. But there was an argument. About me going back East to an art college. I got mad and told him to go to hell, I'd make my own way. I tore up that sketch and stormed out, him yelling all the time. . . .'

Enderby tried hard to get a good look at Renny's face but there wasn't really enough light. Still, he felt the kid was telling the truth: his tone sounded sincere. 'Someone shot your father, Renny. He's in a coma in Painted Rock according to Brewster. . . .' Buck paused. 'Brewster! He let me think he was still a Ranger and that I have to serve out my time! He's a mean cuss. He just might've ridden in on the Senator to square with him for having him fired . . . we'd better move.'

'I'm not going without Rina.'

'Hell, they'll've taken her back to Don Diego by now. Or be well along the trail.'

Renny shook his head, 'No. Seems the Don's coming up to meet them. Something to do with Rina. Heard them say when I was playing dead. They're camped a couple of miles from here, in a canyon with a spring. They don't like to be too far from water out here. . . .'

'How many?'

'Let's see, I killed two, winged another. Be six still in fighting condition.'

'And just you and me go after them? Kid, you're weak as a new fawn . . . and we've only got one horse between us.'

'You can easily wideloop another, you did it before. And I can shoot all right. Set me up with a rifle and I'll pick off every one of those damn Mexes!'

Buck pursed his lips. 'Got a taste for killing, have you?'

He thought Renny flushed. The kid shook his head. 'Not really, but I want Rina.'

'You'll have Don Diego's men stalking you for as long as you're together.'

'We *want* to be together. I know, we're only a couple of kids, but what's that got to do with it? You're twice my age but, tell me, what makes it better for you to marry than for me?'

'Marriage, huh?'

'The works, look, she said she was pregnant and I came here to take her to an old woman I knew who could get rid of the baby. But along the way I had a change of mind. I like the idea of a kid . . . but she . . .'

Buck shook his head. 'Kids bringing up kids!'

'How old was your mother when she had her first kid?' Renny snapped, sounding like his old spoiled self.

Sixteen, according to family lore, but Buck didn't aim

to tell Renny that. Instead, he sighed, helped Pardoe towards his horse and said, 'Let's go, I'm too damn tired to argue and I'm in a hurry to get back to Kim. Brewster was still at her place when I left. . . .'

The Mexicans were gathered around the rock pool fed by the spring, still eating. Enderby and Renny Pardoe could smell the beans and chili and their mouths watered. Renny picked out the girl, a slight figure sitting at one end of a log by herself, eating desultorily.

'She don't look pregnant!' allowed Buck.

'She's not, she only told her father that so he'd disown her, throw her out. Figured it would make it easier for us. She loves me that much . . . but she never told me until we were well on the trail to Gallatera. Now gimme a gun and I'll rake the camp. . . .'

'They're only men doing their job, kid.'

'They left me for dead, for Chrissakes!'

'Obeying orders. Daren't not to. These *rancheros* make their own law. . . .'

'We can't give 'em any kind of a chance! They'll kill Rina!'

'With her father supposedly on his way to see her? Talk sense, kid.'

Renny narrowed his eyes. 'You're back to calling me "kid"!'

'Play this my way and I'll start calling you "Renny" again.'

'You know what you can do!'

'I know I'll put a bullet through your gunhand if

you don't follow orders.'

He heard Renny swallow: the kid knew he meant it and nodded jerkily, muttering, 'All *right*, damn you!'

For once, Renny did as he was told. At the prearranged signal he opened fire, shooting into the group, sending their tin plates spinning, scattering the coals of the fire, lead ripping into the pool. The Mexicans yelled and jumped up and ran for their guns which they had left near a big flat rock. More of Renny's lead spat amongst the weapons, kicking two into the air. The Mexicans stopped dead.

The girl had had enough sense to drop behind the log. Then Buck Enderby rode slowly into the camp, six gun cocked. One man snatched at his waistband and Buck shot him through the shoulder. The others lifted their hands high.

'*Amigos*, no need for anyone to die, Rina, climb up on one of them horses and bring a spare, for Renny.'

Her hair wild, pale face no more than a blurred oval, she gasped. 'Renny! He lives?'

'That's him up on the rim. And he's itching to drop these men one by one.' He grinned at the Mexicans who had rolled their eyes towards the dark rim. 'I think you men should remove your trousers and boots. Rina, you ride up to Renny while I tend to these fellers. They're about to take an unscheduled bath.'

'You will die a horrible death, *gringo*!' hissed a man Buck figured to be the leader as he awkwardly started to remove his boots.

'You'll have to catch me first, *amigo*.' And hard on

his words, as Rina came out of the canyon, leading a horse for Renny, Enderby rode in amongst the remaining mounts shouting and loosing off two shots. As they whirled and raced out of the canyon, he herded the pantless *caballeros* into the pool and made them squat down up to their necks. Then he laughed, yelled, '*Adios, pescados*!'

Their curses and threats rang from the canyon walls as he rowelled his mount away.

The return ride to the Rio was not without its excitement.

Some of the more courageous Gallatera ruffians were waiting even as they came back from the canyon. Obviously, they figured it would be easier to try to take the back-from-the-dead Renny and the young girl from a lone *gringo* rather than from a band of Don Diego's *caballeros.*

They were wrong. The girl had taken a rifle and a pistol from the Mexicans' weapons pile before riding out with the spare mount for Renny. She surprised Enderby when they were chased by the impatient Gallatera men who broke cover instead of allowing the trio to ride into ambush.

Renny and Buck tried to protect her by keeping her between them, but then she slid the rifle from the scabbard on the large Mexican saddle and began shooting. She wasn't too accurate but she was game. She brought down two horses that Buck witnessed and when one of the dismounted men ran to grab her leg, trying to pull her out of the saddle, she had slashed her spur rowel across his face. He dropped away screaming and bloody, and she brought the rifle around and shot him, the blast blowing him clear off his feet.

Buck accounted for three men, one wounded, two dead. Renny said he shot four but Buck didn't figure that kind of a count and wondered if the kid was trying to impress the girl.

Not that it mattered, because they broke free and hit the flats where they gave their mounts their heads. Renny and the girl drew ahead of Enderby because his mount was weary from the long trail down and the hard country didn't make it any easier.

Buck liked Rina Diego. She was sixteen, she said, dark-haired, dark-eyed, with a nose a shade too acquiline for his liking, but her mouth was just right and her friendly smiles transformed her face into something he could only think of as being radiant. She seemed to have more maturity than Renny although he was almost a year older. Her upbringing had been stricter and more confining. No doubt Don Diego and his *institutriz*, the several governesses he employed to teach Rina the various aspects of the life she would be expected to live, had been too rigorous and straitlaced. Being high-spirited, she had rebelled and when the swaggering young Renny had appeared with his sweet-talk and winning ways . . . well, it must have been one hell of a shock to Don Diego.

The *ranchero* would have imposed even nore restrictions on her in the Old Spanish way but found he was banging his head against a stone wall. Buck didn't know Diego but had heard of him and if the daughter was in any way like her father, then it would be two mighty stubborn people at loggerheads.

Inevitably, she had been won over by Renny and then the real trouble had started.

But she had pined for him, had never forgotten him, and had waited for him to keep his promise to return, which, while having been made in haste, he did try to honour. They seemed a happy, well-suited pair to Buck, although he still found himself baulking at their tender ages. However, both had shown they were ready, willing, and able to tackle adult problems and he felt no guilt about leading them away from the Mexican pursuers in a deadly game of hide and seek amongst some of the roughest and most dangerous country on the North American continent.

There was one bunch of *bandidos* close to the Rio that they out-manouevred but had to trade some shots with before they were safely out of danger. Then it was an almost clear run to the Rio.

They reached it just after high noon on a hot, bright day but Enderby held them back when they made ready for the final short ride down to the wide, muddy river.

'We cross at night. This is where I brought you across before, Renny, but it's best done at night.'

'You took me across in broad daylight,' Renny snapped, maybe putting on a show for Rina, letting her see he didn't jump through hoops just on Buck's word.

'Had no choice then and we were lucky. There're few patrols out here because it's so rugged and isolated, but I know just where the ford is. You go plunging in and miss, you'll be in water forty feet deep with ugly currents. We'll make it over tonight and then head for Del Rio in Texas, skirting Villa Acuna on this side. They sometimes have rurales stationed there.'

The girl gave him a quizzical look, one he had noted she used pretty often. She didn't always follow through with questions, but this time she did. 'You seem to know the border well, Señor Buck . . . Yet Renny tells me you came from a long way off.'

'Tennessee, ' Buck admitted. 'Yeah, long way from here, but I did a lot of border work after the war ended.'

She looked at Renny and smiled, her face softening. 'Then I think we should not argue with Buck, Renny, *querido mio*.'

Renny looked a might sullen but nodded in bad grace. 'If that's the way you want it, Rina. ' He slightly emphasized the "you" and her smile looked mischievous.

They followed Buck Enderby and he led them safely across the river. They reached Del Rio sometime after nine o'clock and went into the *Rialito* diner on a street that ran down towards the river. A tall man, eating at a table with another man and two women, glanced up, paused with his fork halfway to his mouth. He wore a Van Dyke beard and moustache, nodded slightly, but no one in Buck's group seemed to know him.

They were eating well enough when they heard the stomp of heavy boots coming down the room.

Several other customers watched as a small, tight group of dusty men came towards the table where Enderby and his friends sat.

It was Brewster, Chip Riley, and Trapper.

CHAPTER 12

HOME ON THE RANGE

They were all wearing their Texas Ranger badges and the other customers murmured amongst themselves, setting down knives and forks, watching, wondering if there was going to be trouble.

Buck Enderby was wondering the same thing and he set his own cutlery down quietly. The girl didn't know Brewster or his men but immediately sensed danger from the way Renny and Buck were acting.

Brewster smiled, touched a hand to his hat in Rina's direction and lifted his other hand in friendly gesture.

'No need to get excited, folks. Just a friendly call.'

But as he held their attention for a few seconds, Trapper swung a sawn-off shotgun into view from behind his back and the double hammers ratchetted back, the sound loud in the hushed diner. Chip Riley brought up his six-gun, hammer cocked.

'Your idea of friendly and mine don't seem to match up, Cord,' Buck said slowly, aware of the other diners staring, frozen in their chairs.

Brewster made a 'sorry, but what can you do about it' gesture with his hands and then his Colt appeared in the blink of an eye. 'Renny Pardoe, I arrest you for the attempted murder of your father, Senator Pardoe, of Painted Rock, Texas. By now it could even be a "murder" charge.'

'I never shot him!' Renny shouted, jumping to his feet in his excitement, but Rina's calming hand reached up for his and tugged gently. Slowly, he sat down, eyes hot and wild. 'Will . . . will the . . . Senator make it?'

Brewster shrugged. 'Buck, old pard, I'm gonna have to take you in, too, for aiding and abetting this young hellion.'

'I brought him back to Texas for you, didn't I?' Buck said. Shock and anger washed over Renny's face, but Rina spoke quietly in his ear and he calmed down some, though still on edge, raging for action.

Brewster shook his head at Buck. 'Sorry, it don't work that way. If I didn't know from your earlier report which part of the Rio you were gonna cross, you'd have taken the kid to Painted Rock and then, likely, wherever he wanted to go if the Senator didn't make it. You're in this deep, *amigo.*' He touched the old scar on his cheek and his face hardened. 'Things you've done go back a long way and it's about time they caught up with you.'

Enderby watched him coldly. 'You're fooling no one, Cord. I know the Senator fired you and these two snakes, as well as Brosnan and Conner.'

'Well, I was you, I'd behave myself anyway, Buck –

Bud an' Con're still out there with Kim, keepin' an eye on things, you might say . . . we'll be joinin' 'em soon. Good place to hole-up while we I negotiate with Don Diego and the Senator.'

Renny snapped his head up. 'Thought you said he was dying?'

'Did I? Well, he could be, but I don't think he'll die before we make some arrangements about payin' a big ransom for you, and Diego will no doubt pay a bigger one for the *senorita* here.'

Rina's eyes were cold as she levelled her gaze at Brewster. 'I am sorry to disappoint you, senor. My father has disowned me. He will not now acknowledge my existence, so I think you will not collect any ransom, big or small.'

Brewster frowned, something in the girl's tone and her confidence shook him. He looked at Buck. 'What's she talkin' about? Them old *rancheros*'ll rip the world apart if it means savin' one of their precious off-spring, specially a gal, and a looker like her. . . .'

'There's a complication, Cord,' Enderby said calmly and told Brewster about it in a low voice. The other tensed customers, afraid to move, strained to hear.

When Buck had finished, Brewster swore, he knew Enderby wasn't lying. Then he brightened.

'Well, I can still do some kinda deal, I'll collect from the Senator first, then tell Don Diego I'll throw in Renny's head, long as he pays up for the gal . . . bet he'll be glad to see the kid dead.'

'You're a worse snake than I figured, Cord,'

Enderby said, anger boiling up in him and he started to his feet.

Brewster's gun fired instantly, and Buck was hurled back against the wall violently, blood on his shirt front. He half-twisted and fell on his side, dragging his chair down with him. The women customers screamed and one fainted. Rina covered her face with her hands. Renny narrowed his eyes.

'You're a dead man, mister!' he told Brewster.

'Got that wrong, kid. Buck's the dead 'un.'

Brewster swung his gun and it cracked against the kid's head. The impact was only partially absorbed by the neckerchief still tied around Renny's head, and he sprawled across Rina's lap and then spilled off to the floor. She knelt beside him swiftly, talking anxiously in Spanish.

Brewster swung around as one of the male diners came up hesitantly. 'What d'you want?'

'Sir, I am a doctor. I think that man you shot may need . . . attention.' It was the man with the Van Dyke beard.

'Not if I shot him. Trap, cover the room while Chip drags the kid out.' He took the girl by the arm and frowned as the doctor knelt beside the still Enderby and half-turned him on his back. 'Well?'

The doctor's face was pale when he looked at Brewster. 'Unfortunately, sir, you are right. This man is past all needs now, your bullet has seen to that.'

Brester kind of sneered as he looked down at Enderby's body. His left hand rubbed gently at the scar on his face. 'Well, I ain't gonna miss him, all right, boys, let's light out of here right now. You folk stay put, this is official Ranger business. You interfere and you'll end up in more trouble then you ever dreamed of, c'mon *move*!'

The group had passed through the doorway and out into the night before Enderby groaned and twitched a little.

The doctor, halfway to his feet, stopped and spoke sharply to a waiter who had come hurrying up.

'Get me hot water and some cloths! Quickly, man!'

The waiter hesitated fractionally and then sped off. As the doctor rolled Enderby on to his back, one of the men he had been dining with walked across.

'You said the man was dead, Franklin!'

The doctor smiled as he opened Enderby's shirt and revealed that the bullet had cut through the big chest muscle, burned his arm and then slapped into the wall. There was a knot on Buck's head where it had struck a chair as he fell. The sawbones pointed to it.

'Lucky the fall knocked him out or that so-called Ranger would've put a finishing shot into him.' He staunched the flow of blood from the wound with a clean handkerchief, looking around for the tardy waiter who was just coming from the direction of the kitchen now with towels and a bowl of steaming water. Doctor Bryce Franklin gave his puzzled friend a half-smile.

'I know this man, he once saved my life. Seemed the only decent thing to do on my part tonight was to reciprocate . . . Now, lend a hand here, Sol . . .'

'You are completely mad, sir! Here I save your life for

you and now you intend to risk it by – by riding a hundred miles, into an inevitable gunfight!'

Doctor Franklin was genuinely angry as Enderby swung his legs slowly over the side of the narrow bed in the small infirmary. He sat there, head swimming, breathing a little harder than usual, swathes of bandage wrapped about his chest.

'Doc, we're square now, but I have to go, Brewster's gonna ransom those two kids, and he'll kill them as soon as he collects the money.'

Franklin sighed, started for the door. 'I'll get you a clean shirt. One of mine should fit—' He paused. 'It was a long time ago that you rode up and saved my wife and I from those bandits, Buck. You've aged and you're showing it, but I guess that you're no less tough than you were in those days.'

Enderby, struggling with his trousers, paused, looking sober. 'I'm tough enough, Doc.'

Franklin nodded. 'Buck, this is a foolish thing you do, although I understand why a man like you has to do it even at great risk. If you know where they are taking the young people, couldn't you get help from the Law?'

'Call in the Rangers, maybe?'

Franklin nodded slowly. 'Yes, I see, you *have* to do this yourself. Even when I knew you before, you struck me as an honourable man, *that* certainly hasn't changed. I'll get that shirt for you.'

Buck nodded, breathing heavily now from his efforts at dressing, wondering if he would be able to make it all the way to Kim's ranch.

*

Brewster was so confident that he hadn't even placed a guard to watch the approaches to the ranch.

None that Enderby could see, anyway, from where he lay up in the mesquite on a ledge overlooking the house and yard. Kim's ranch hands were nowhere to be seen but Brewster would have made sure she sent them far afield on chores that would keep them away from the ranch house.

He still wasn't completely sure Conner had told him the truth about there being no guards, but he was prepared to risk it. He'd already risked plenty riding out here and the bandages under his borrowed shirt felt wet.

Coming through Snake Pass, named for its twisting shape rather than any denizen of the reptile world that inhabited its confines, Buck Enderby had seen a man with a rifle running for the cover of some rocks up on the slope. He had recognized Conner, the fifth man in Brewster's gang, and a back-shooter from way back.

Without hesitation, Buck threw his rifle to his shoulder and triggered, but the movement of his damaged chest muscles made him flinch and he missed. Dirt erupted a foot in front of Conner's boots. The man slipped and slid back two yards, dust shrouding him.

Gritting his teeth, Buck levered and held the rifle raised and ready. When the dust thinned, he saw that Conner had rolled on to his back, rifle across his body. The gun blasted and Enderby heard the *thrrrrruppp!* of the bullet passing overhead. He fired and levered again, but it was too much for his chest and the rifle sagged and wavered wildly.

Not that it mattered. Conner was hit, dropped his own gun and rolled and slid to the bottom of the slope. Buck heeled his mount across and stopped the horse almost on top of the man as he writhed and sobbed in agony. The bullet had passed through his chest, side to side, and he didn't have long. Enderby put a shot into the ground by the man's head, wrenching a cry from him. He looked up with fear-filled, dulling eyes.

'Tell me Brewster's set-up, Con, do it quick. You ain't got long.'

'Go . . . to . . . hell!' The man coughed blood, stiffened when Buck levered a shell into the breech.

'Con, you're dying. You're in bad pain now. But I can make it a lot worse before you breathe your last.' He aimed the rifle at the man's right knee cap. 'Now, about Brewster's set-up at Kim's place. . . .'

Conner had told all he knew which mainly came down to the fact that Brewster was holding both Renny and Rina for ransom, but that he thought Buck was dead and as far as Con knew there were no guards.

Now it seemed as if the dying killer had told the truth. He had been on his way to send the ransom notes to the Senator and Don Diego when he had spotted Buck coming into Snake Pass and thought to bushwhack him. He should have just hidden and allowed Enderby to ride on through.

Now there was one less for Buck to tackle at the ranch.

It was late afternoon and he figured he would wait

until dusk – when they would likely be at supper – or even full dark. Likely Kim's men had been told to camp out for the night. If they came back, Buck would have some allies, but he didn't think it likely that Brewster would chance having a bunkhouse full of loyal cowboys close by.

He had felt a hell of a lot better than he did right now, as he hitched around trying to get comfortable, the ache in his chest was rising into his neck and head, creeping down his bullet-burned left arm into his fingers which he could hardly bend enough to grip the fore-end of the rifle firmly.

He would just have to use his Colt, which would give him only six shots, and four men to take down with them, four *unwounded* men, all intent on killing him.

Kim, Renny, and Rina would be in danger, too. If he couldn't work it so that they were out of the line of fire, well, he didn't want to think about that.

Diversion. That's what he needed. He was waiting in brush not far from the corrals and as the shadows closed down he moved closer, crouched almost double and nearly stepped on a sleeping rattlesnake, enjoying the cooling air, no doubt. He hated snakes but they were a fact of life out here and a man had to learn to live with them. Running a tongue around his lips, he started to edge past, then stopped, took several deep breaths, watching the snake, crouched slowly, biting back on the pain it caused him. His right palm was sweating already as he let it hover over the snake's head. The beady, lidless eyes seemed to be watching him and he knew that the reptile's instincts would waken it any moment. As it started to lift a little from the coiled body, he grabbed, managing to get a thumb over the top of the head, holding the jaws closed. The snake writhed and rattled furiously and, heart thundering, Buck stood unsteadily in the brush and hurled the snake into the midst of the horses in the corral.

There was instant pandemonium. The startled snake struck wildly as it landed on the back of a big dappled grey and, slithering off, bit into the belly of a sorrel. Horses reared and shrilled and screamed, pawing the air, retreating, eyes wild, snorting as they plunged, striking frantically at the terrified snake with their hoofs while it only wanted to get away from this instant hell.

The front door burst open and Chip Riley and Trapper came out on to the porch, Trapper with sawn-off shotgun braced against his hip.

'What the hell's wrong?' called Brewster from inside the house.

'Jesus!' yelled Riley who was ahead of Trapper as they ran towards the corrals. 'Rattler!'

'Christ is that all,' growled Brewster. 'Kill the damn thing then. . . .'

Riley drew his sixgun, dancing aside with boots spread wide. He triggered wildly and Trapper yelled.

'Goddamnit! That bullet tore through my pants leg!' Then the shotgun roared and when it did, Buck fired from his bush, the shotgun's thunder covering the sound of his Colt. 'I got him! That fixed the son of a bitch. . . ! No, he's still wrigglin'!'

Trapper hesitated, about to shoot, but suddenly

aware that Chip Riley was staring at him wide-eyed, with a stream of blood flowing out of his sagging mouth. Then as Riley's legs gave way under him Trapper saw Enderby in the bushes and he shouted a curse and swung the gun up and around.

Buck dropped flat, shooting, and the bush above him was torn to pieces, sap and chewed bark raining down on him. Trapper had fallen through the bars of the corral where the horses were still milling, one down from the snake's bite, the rest calming. He was trampled underfoot and as Enderby tried to push to his feet, fat Bud Brosnan stumbled out on to the porch.

'Sounds like a goddamn war! What the hell're you—' He cut whatever he was going to say, dragging at his Colt. 'Cord! Cord! Enderby's out here!'

He was throwing himself sideways even as he spoke, gun hammering. Buck's leg gave under him and he slipped, put out his left hand to keep from falling flat and cried aloud as the searing pain shot through him. He rolled half on to his back as lead tore at the thin brush.

Brosnan was shooting through the porch rails and Buck's bullet tore a long sliver of wood, sending it humming and spinning. It struck Brosnan on the ear, ripping it partly from his head. He clapped a hand over the bloody wound and half-raised up, cursing in his agony.

His head jerked violently as Buck's next bullet took him through the temple and he fell, kicking jerkily, as Brewster appeared in the doorway. He was holding a gun, but the barrel was pressed into the thick hair covering Kim Preece's head.

'I dunno how you did it, Buck, but you've lost out anyway! I guess I don't have to spell it out!'

Enderby, still crouching, said nothing. His head was whirling and it hurt like hell to breathe. His left arm was useless and he thought he only had one bullet left in the Colt. Maybe none. He had lost count.

Which only added to the danger both he and Kim were in. Brewster had yanked her head back so that her neck was stretched, and her face was contorted in pain.

Slowly, Enderby started to stand. He stumbled twice and he saw Brewster tense, ready to shoot. He raised his right hand holding the Colt, left arm dangling, his shirt front red with his blood. His face looked ghastly, grey and lined and dirt-smeared.

'Let it drop, Buck!' rapped Brewster and Enderby released his hold on the Colt.

He swayed unsteadily. 'Kim's not in this, Cord.'

'That a fact?' Brewster grinned and shook the woman. 'Looks like she's in it from where I'm standin', but *you* ain't in it any longer! Figured I'd finished with you, but I'll do that right now and then make myself a rich man. . . .'

Then there was a high-pitched scream from in the house and Brewster whirled even as something moved in a blur and he and Kim and Renny Pardoe, hands tied behind him, all thrashed together on the porch. Brewster dropped his pistol, dazed by the impact of Renny's body. Kim writhed out from under as Renny rolled on to his back and kicked savagely at

Brewster, sending him crashing into the wall.

He snarled and came back at the kid, punching him in the face, whipping out his hunting knife. Then Kim, sobbing, picked up the Colt and lifted it in both hands as she triggered.

Brewster staggered, looking around with a shocked expression. She fired again. He slammed into the wall, looking down at the blood spurting from his body. Then his eyes rolled up into his head and he fell on his face, unmoving.

Renny Pardoe was comforting Rina, who seemed little the worse for her rough experiences, while Kim poured iodine into Enderby's wound, making him squirm.

'Glad of your help, Renny,' he said quietly. 'Seems some of what I taught you about thinking of someone apart from yourself has rubbed-off.'

The kid shrugged. 'Maybe . . . I moved before I knew what I was doing.'

'That's what I mean, it was instinctive.'

Rina prodded Renny. 'He did it deliberately, Señor Buck! Told me to scream so as to startle Brewster. . . .' She smiled fondly at him and moved closer. 'I think he is a good *hombre*!'

'Yeah, he's not bad,' Buck conceded quietly and Renny grinned slowly.

'Well, seems Brewster lied about the Senator. He wasn't shot at all. Just wanted you to get after me. Taking me hostage was to be his way of getting back at the Senator.'

Buck looked at him narrowly. 'The Senator . . . ?'

Renny nodded, still smiling. 'Yeah, you know: my father.'

Buck nodded approval. 'Reckon he'll be happy with his new daughter-in-law, too.' Winking at Rina, he turned to Kim who had hardly spoken since the gunfight. 'I'll get on the trail come morning.'

She tied off the bandage and looked at him soberly. 'Now why would you do that? Why would you want to leave again so soon? You're home now, Buck Enderby. Home!' She smiled and added, 'I don't know what I'd do if I didn't have you to patch up every now and again, anyway.'

It sounded good to him.